Sunday, Monday, and Always

Sunday, Monday, and Always

DAWN POWELL

INTRODUCTION AND FURTHER
SELECTION BY TIM PAGE

STEERFORTH PRESS
SOUTH ROYALTON, VERMONT

The stories included in this collection were originally published in:
Collier's ("Audition"); *Esquire* ("Dinner on the Rocks");
Hearst's International Cosmopolitan ("Every Day is Ladies' Day"
and "Adam); *Mademoiselle* ("Feet on the Ground," "Here Today,
Gone Tomorrow," and "Cheerio"); *The New Yorker* ("Blue Hyacinths,"
"Artist's Life," "Such a Pretty Day," "Can't We Cry a Little," and
"The Comeback"); the *Saturday Evening Post* ("The Elopers");
Story Magazine, Inc. ("You Should Have Brought Your Mink"
and "Ideal Home"); and *Today's Woman* ("The Grand March"
and "Deenie"); *Vogue* ("What are You Doing in My Dreams").

Library of Congress Cataloging-in-Publication Data

Powell, Dawn.
Sunday, Monday, and always / Dawn Powell :
introduction by Tim Page — Rev. ed.
p. cm.
ISBN 1–883642–60–4 (alk. paper)
1. United States—Social life and customs—20th century Fiction.
2. Manhattan (New York, N.Y.)—Social life and customs Fiction.
3. Ohio—Social life and customs Fiction.   I. Title.
PS3531.0936S86   1999
13'.52—dc21   99-43312
CIP

Manufactured in the United States of America
FIRST PAPERBACK EDITION

CONTENTS

Introduction

𝒟AWN POWELL WROTE short stories through-
out her life—at least one hundred of them have been identified
already and that figure is undoubtedly on the conservative side.

Strange as it may seem today, there was once a considerable—
and lucrative—market available to writers who could tell a tight,
interesting story in just a few pages. Powell saw her stories printed
not only in *The New Yorker, Mademoiselle, Story,* and the *Saturday
Evening Post* but in what are now obscure and only dimly remembered venues, such as *Snappy Stories* and *Munsey's.*

She published short stories for almost fifty years from her
debut effort—"Phyllis Takes Care of the Children," in the *Lake
Erie Record* (1915) through the wrenching "The Elopers," which
appeared in the *Saturday Evening Post* two years before she died.

If short-story writing came easily to Powell, it did not necessarily come naturally. In all of her work, she fought off a ten-
dency to overwrite, and she seems to have found this clipped,

tautly controlled genre restrictive. After all, much of her best writing always went into inspired digressions from her plots and such a method was not suited to the traditional short-story form, which has room for few, if any, meanderings.

Moreover, throughout most of her career, Powell thought of the genre primarily as a way of making money to help her get on with what she considered her "real work"—her novels and (for a while, at least) her plays. And so, much of the time, one senses that the writing of short stories was a necessary distraction for Powell—better paid than book-reviewing, to be sure, and less hassled and formula-bound than writing for the movies, but a distraction nonetheless.

For example, in 1933, when she made her initial sale to *The New Yorker*—a cherished objective for most writers, then as now—Powell was dismissive, albeit a little amazed. "That little gadget I wrote sold to *New Yorker* for seventy dollars," she marveled in her diary. "Having failed completely in all serious work, barely getting a reputation for average, let alone anything else—with this encouragement in the far-too-easy-for-me light touch I believe I may change—see what I have, inasmuch as it seems to be superior of its slight kind—and be opportunistic from now on."

That "gadget," entitled "Such a Pretty Day," is in the present volume. It was the earliest of Powell's stories that she admitted into the collection called *Sunday, Monday, and Always* published by Houghton Mifflin in 1952—the only gathering from her voluminous short fiction issued during her lifetime.

Powell assembled *Sunday, Monday, and Always* during a prolonged bout of writer's block that lasted, in varying degrees of severity, for a five-year period that began just after the publication of *The Locusts Have No King* in 1948 and continued through 1953, when she managed to begin her final assault on the long-promised, long-delayed *The Wicked Pavilion*.

On several occasions, Powell had suggested a volume of this sort to Scribners, which published all of her books through the 1940s. In 1951, when the idea was turned down yet again, Powell took it personally and left the firm. Her friend Rosalind Baker Wilson brought her to the Boston-based Houghton Mifflin, which was more than happy to bring out Powell's omnibus. The author then began to read through and evaluate the short fiction she had written over the decades. Among these, she found only eighteen stories she deemed worthy of inclusion (although she later made up a list of another eighteen that might make up a second collection).

It was during a luncheon with Wilson, who would be Powell's editor throughout her three-book tenure with Houghton Mifflin, that the book was named. Powell often had difficulty with titles (*The Locusts Have No King* was almost called "Prudentius Psychomania") and Wilson suggested a line from a song that was then playing on the jukebox—"Sunday, Monday, and Always."

"To my shock, Dawn loved the title," Wilson recalled in 1999. "It was just a spontaneous idea of mine—almost a joke—and I immediately tried to retract it because I thought we could do better. But Dawn had made up her mind and *Sunday, Monday, and Always* it was."

The slim book was issued in June 1952. The reviews were excellent in their way, although many critics used the occasion to praise Powell's work in general rather than to laud these particular stories. In *The New York Times,* for example, Orville Prescott ticked off seven stories as "excellent," six as "good," and only five as "ordinary"—not an especially impressive tally for somebody who had been publishing for thirty-five years. In the *New York Post* Malcom Cowley, an old friend who would eventually become Powell's editor for *The Golden Spur,* was generally appreciative but begged for "more relief from these creeps, drips, jerks, phonies, fussbudgets, finaglers, and fuddy-duddies."

Perhaps William Peden, in the *Saturday Review,* came closest to the truth. He cheered Powell's ability to be "entertaining without becoming trivial.... Beneath their facades of boredom and suavity, bar people are naive, provincial, and essentially rather decent human beings," Peden continued. "The author seldom flogs or flays them. She likes them and is kind to them."

We have opted to let Powell's original selection stand. Therefore, this reissue of *Sunday, Monday, and Always* is exactly as the author assembled it (complete with her obscurely motivated division of the stories into three parts).

However, Powell lived on for another thirteen years, during which she published at least two short masterpieces—the autobiographical essay "What Are You Doing in My Dreams?" and "The Elopers," based on the author's own experiences with her much loved, much troubled son, the late Joseph R. Gousha Jr. After we added these concentrated and powerful works, it was decided to throw in a bright early sketch from *The New Yorker,* "Can't We Cry a Little?," and one of Powell's last send-up of domestic foibles, "Dinner on the Rocks," as a sort of appendix.

It is my opinion that Powell's skills as a short-story writer grew as she got older. "The Roof" and "The Glads," which have been cited as among the strongest stories in this book, are remarkably grim and tough-minded vignettes that were rejected by every magazine publisher who saw them and only saw light when they appeared in *Sunday, Monday, and Always.*

Powell never really discovered a way to be "completely opportunistic;" when she was writing purely for hire, she was rarely writing at her best. Despite her initial seventy-dollar windfall, Powell would receive enough rejection letters from *The New Yorker* over the years to paper a small room.

"The Secret of My Failure," she headed a 1956 diary entry. "Just thought why I don't sell stories to popular magazines. All have subtitles—'Last time Gary saw Cindy she was a gawky child; now she was a beautiful woman. . .' I can't help writing, 'Last time Fatso saw Myrt she was a desirable woman; now she was an old bag."

For those of us who are just as comfortable with the Fatsos and Myrts of the world as we are with idealized Garys and Cindys, these sharp, endearing, and humane sketches continue to appeal.

TIM PAGE
MARCH 17, 1999
NEW YORK CITY

PART I

You Should Have Brought Your Mink

You OUGHT TO CALL ON Aunt Mag today," her mother said, as indeed she had said the minute Edna got in the house. "It would break her heart to hear you'd come home without seeing her."

"I will, Mother," Edna said patiently. "Just let me get a little rest first."

"Mothah! Mothah! Did you get that?" mocked sister Claire. "first it's tomahtahs, now it's Mothah deah."

"Will you stop nagging at her, now?" the older sister, Irene, demanded. "A person doesn't get home for twelve years and then you got to nag, nag, nag. If I was Edna I'd never come home."

"You said something," Edna said, but she wasn't going to lose her temper, because she'd be gone in another week and this time she'd like them to remember nice things about her. They expected her to be high-hat but she was going to surprise them for once, show them that she'd had a little good sense knocked into her. She wasn't going to brag and if the place was even shabbier than she remembered it she was not going to carp. It would probably be the last visit she'd make home for another dozen years and there mustn't be any bitterness. She was going to act as if living in New York and being an actress—when she *was* an actress—was no better than being cashier in a village bakery, like Irene, or being waitress in a little railroad hotel like Claire. (Yes, and she might be doing just one of those things herself if she hadn't followed that ham actor's stock company all the way to Pittsburgh! That's how you get ahead, by being a little fool!)

The two sisters were unpacking Edna's trunk, which had just arrived.

"I nearly got one of those myself last year," Irene said, hanging up a little ocelot jacket in the closet, "but then they got so common."

"I thought Edna said she had a mink," Claire said.

"I didn't bring it because I didn't need it on the road," Edna explained.

"I wish you had, though," Irene said. "I sure wish you had."

"Is it real or is it a kind of fabric?" Claire asked.

"It cost sixteen hundred and fifty bucks if that's what you mean," Edna said, and then wished she hadn't said it because she would be hearing this all the time. The girls would tell everybody, "She has a mink coat, genuine, that cost sixteen hundred and fifty dollars." And then the callers would look skeptical and you would hear them thinking it: Well, if she really has it, where is it? I don't notice her wearing it.

"I wish you'd brought it," said her mother. "I'd just like to see Aunt Mag's face when you walked in wearing it."

"Edna's ashamed of Aunt Mag," Claire teased, "that's why she puts off seeing her."

"Now, Claire!" Edna protested, but it was true.

"There's Tub Phillips coming up the walk," her mother said, looking out the window. "He heard you're back. He even keeps that picture of you that was in the paper."

"Which picture?" asked Edna, playfully. "It's always in the papers."

"It was just once in the *Gazette,*" her mother said. "That's the only paper people here read."

"You sent us that piece from Chicago about that play," Claire said. "But we didn't show Tubby because it said you were only fair."

"Maybe they gave you too much to learn," her mother consoled.

Irene went downstairs to let Tub in while Edna fixed her hair. The little rickety bedroom with the big double bed and the single one at the window was the same, it seemed to her, as it had been when they had all shared it as kids. The walnut dressing table with pink scarf had the same collection of perfumes, powders, and brushes to be rigorously kept separate and there was still the big silver hand mirror to be quarreled over. Edna was surprised to find herself so sentimental over these old familiar touches. She hadn't realized she had been so homesick. When she decided on this surprise visit she had thought only of the delight of the family, but she was the one that was getting the thrill out of the shabby old place. It was like old times having Tubby Phillips waiting downstairs. Poor old Tubby that she used to tease so! She felt like rushing down and telling him she was sorry.

"Go ahead, take your time," Claire said, as Edna dropped the comb and brush. "Or is that the way you always wear your hair?"

Mrs. Tompson, who had been finishing the unpacking job, emerged from the closet and cocked her head critically to study Edna.

"Claire, why don't you fix Edna's hair like yours while she's home?" she finally suggested. "Claire has a professional touch."

"But I don't like it frizzy," Edna said.

"Okay." Claire shrugged. "I was just thinking like Mom that a little curl in it would kinda be softening."

"It would take five years off your face," said her mother. "Never mind, though, if you don't want to."

As in the old days when she wanted to avoid further discussion Mrs. Tompson burst out into an old Sunday school song, "You in Your Small Corner, and I in Mine," and it made Edna laugh. She put her arm around her mother's small shoulders going downstairs.

"Ask Tubby to take you over to the Kimble place," Mrs. Tompson whispered. "His sister works there and they could show you over it sometime when the Kimbles are out. It's beautiful."

"Mother, if I call on the natives it won't be when they're out," Edna said with a wry smile, "or by the back door. Please!"

The sight of Tubby Phillips warmed her, for he had patiently dogged her footsteps from kindergarten to high school. His vest buttons were still ready to pop and his pale blue eyes were still worshipful.

"Gee!" he said, getting up. "Gee, Edna. Gee."

This was more like the kind of welcome she had expected and it touched Edna. The family had been amazingly matter-of-fact, she thought.

"Well, Edna, you married yet?"

That was the question everyone had asked.

"I guess Edna's just too particular," her mother defended her. "She's got a beau all right in New York, judging by all the telegrams she's been getting from this Mr. Aldine."

"I thought she said he was married," said Claire.

"Let's see," said Tub, "are you the one that's thirty on April fifth or is it Claire. We were figuring out."

"Me," said Claire. "Edna's thirty-three and Irene's thirty-five. Edna's going on thirty-three and a half."

"Let's talk about something pleasant," Edna said.

"That's right," said Tub. "Well, we none of us get any younger, do we? Gee, you must have done mighty well to stay away from home all this time. Still interested in the stage?"

"That's my job," Edna said, smiling. "I just finished a tour in Chicago, and that's why I'm here for a little rest. Didn't you ever hear about a show called *Like Sisters*? My goodness!"

"Ever meet Rosalie Stanford in the city?" Tub inquired. "She's from near here. She's on the radio."

Claire had an inspiration.

"Tub, why don't you ask Mrs. Kimble to give Edna a letter of introduction to Rosalie when she goes back?"

"That's right," agreed Mrs. Tompson, wagging her head over her knitting. "She might be able to do something for you, Edna. There's no reason why she couldn't introduce you to some radio people."

"Heavens, Mother, I know plenty of them!" Edna exclaimed.

"I mean the big shots, though," said Claire.

"I could speak to Mrs. Kimble, sure," said Tub, "when I go over to fix the roof tomorrow. Have you seen your Aunt Mag yet? Say, I'll bet she gets a kick out of having a niece from New York City visit her!"

"She'll never stop talking about it," said Claire. "It'll be all over Shantyville."

A sudden old memory brought a cloud to Edna's face.

"Do they still call this end of town Shantyville?" she asked. "Even since they've paved it and made the park?"

"Can't break the habit," Tub chuckled. "Long as this is the Irish end this'll be Shantyville, paved or not."

"This evening, Edna," said her mother, pleadingly. "Why don't you run over to Aunt Mag's tonight? Just let her have a breath of New York, you know she's never been anywhere."

"Three hundred pounds and stone-deaf," said Tub.

It was time for Irene to report to the bakery and she came in now with her coat on. On Saturdays she went at eleven and worked till midnight.

"Here's that clipping from last night's paper," she told Edna, and handed her a piece of paper, which Edna read out loud.

Miss Edna Tompson, formerly of this city and now of the stage, is visiting her mother Mrs. Minnie Tompson, widow of Pete Tompson for many years a popular handyman around town.

"Handyman, my eye!" muttered Mrs. Tompson. "If you call it handyman standing in front of Brier's saloon twenty-four hours a day."

"Oh, Mother!" Edna expostulated.

"Mothah, Mothah!" Claire repeated. "There it goes again."

"Am I supposed to go through life saying 'bejaber' 'cause Papa and Aunt Mag did?" Edna snapped, and then was sorry, for her mother gave an embarrassed laugh saying, "Still got her temper, hasn't she?"

"Tell Tub about meeting Mrs. Cary's daughter on the train and how nice she was to you," Mrs. Tompson urged. "She came right up to Edna and spoke, Tubby. Believe me, if I get any sewing to do for Mrs. Cary this winter I'm going to tell her how much I appreciate that."

"She's seen me in the show in Chicago, that's all," said Edna. "She wanted my autograph."

"There's nothing snobbish about the Carys," said Mrs. Tompson. "I always said that. It's 'howdoyoudo, Mrs. Tompson' every time I meet one of them, even Paul, the one in the bank."

"I suppose you heard about the Davis girl," said Tub, "the one you used to run with."

"Those Davis girls were a disgrace to the neighborhood," declared Mrs. Tompson. "Thank God not one of my girls ever got in trouble. I don't count that little squirt walking out on my Claire after six months, because they were really married, I can show you the license."

"Ah, Mom!" Claire pouted.

"Alma Davis," said Edna, "that was my friend."

"You and Alma used to have some high old times, believe me," Claire recollected. "Irene and Mom used to go nearly crazy waiting for you. Mom, remember the time they hennaed their hair?"

"We were just kids," said Edna. "Alma was all right."

"The worst one of the lot, that was Alma," stated Mrs. Tompson. "I was glad when she ran away."

Tub got his hat and stood up.

"I got the Kimbles' car out there, maybe you'd like me to show you the West side of town. Some beautiful new homes out there," he said.

Edna smiled at him, detesting him just like in old days. It was funny how you thought you could stay away from home twelve years and get a detached feeling, but as soon as you hung up your hat there again you were sucked into the old world, all the old feeling.

"Thanks, Tub," she said, "but I'll stay right here in Shantyville this trip. I'm just resting."

"I'll be going past your Aunt Mag's," he said. "It would sure be a treat for her if you dropped in right now while she's fixing dinner."

"All right," said Edna, and got her coat.

"You should have brought the mink," sighed her mother.

One thing about the house was that Irene had done away with the old ashcan and sunflower yard and planted bushes and a hedge. That was something.

"Tell her all about the stage," her mother called from the door as Tub and Claire and Edna got in the car. "Tell her about New York. Aunt Mag isn't going to last long, it'll tickle her."

If the Tompson's little house was improved in the past decade Aunt Mag's was worse than ever, a two-room tumble-down shack by the freight yards with a chicken shed and a half-dozen scrawny Plymouth Rocks flapping around in a barbed-wire enclosure. You never remembered people being poor, you only remembered things like the other kids making fun of Aunt Mag as a town character.

She was sitting in her little parlor with the shades down when they walked in, her eyes closed in a little catnap while a radio skit came roaring out of a harmless-looking little box on the table.

"That's Rosalie Stanford's program," said Claire. "'The Brave Little Widow.' She's the daughter in it."

"Well, Edna!" cackled Aunt Mag, hugging her. "I declare I wouldn't have known you. Well, you can't live that life and not have it show, they tell me. Sit down, sit down."

The bed with its patchwork-quilt covering took up a large part of the room, so the three guests sat down there in a row facing Aunt Mag who seemed permanently wedged into her carpet-seated rocker.

"What's new?" she cried. "Are you still a good girl? Are you on the stage on Broadway, New York? Do you sing songs and dance? Speak up, I'm a little deaf. No, no, leave the radio be, there, that don't bother."

It was a task to speak up over the radio voices but the confusion of noises did not bother Aunt Mag, so Edna tried it.

"I just say lines, Aunt Mag," she said. "Of course I'm not a leading lady but I get by, sometimes a bit and sometimes a really good part. This last play for instance—"

Edna was surprised to find that at last she was having the kind of welcome she had wanted, someone she could tell the funny little things that had happened in the show, the little jealousies, the little triumphs, and here was Aunt Mag drinking it all in, rocking and nodding her head, the only person, when you came to think of it, who was really glad to see her, the only person really interested. Aunt Mag might be a fat old cleaning woman who couldn't read or write but she at least had a little imagination beyond the neighborhood or village, you could talk to her and you got sympathy. Claire, for instance, got up as soon as Edna began talking and went out to talk to some young fellows in the freight office. Claire, who was supposed to be so smart because she finished high school! She came back in smoking a cigarette after a while.

"Did I miss anything?" she asked gaily.

Aunt Mag's round, ruddy face turned to her excitedly.

"You missed the best part, Claire," she exclaimed. "You missed the trial scene. They got her on the stand, they found the revolver in her coat pocket, remember yesterday, then they began heckling her because she was only a widow, then this Lawyer Purvis, the one that's her friend but she don't know it, he takes her part, he comes in with the daughter—"

"Oh, was Rosalie in it today?" Claire asked. "Oh I wish I'd stayed to listen, but I thought Edna was talking. Oh darn."

"Your Aunt Mag ain't so deaf," chuckled Tubby. "Hears every word that comes off that program."

"They take her to the hospital tomorrow—" said Aunt Mag.

"Who?" Claire interrupted eagerly. "The Brave Little Widow or the daughter?"

"The daughter," said Aunt Mag. "They're going to see if she recognizes the body or will its weeks in the river have swollen it beyond recognition. Now turn to KDKA, Tubby."

"Well, I got to get to work," Claire said. "Come on, Edna, unless you want to talk to Aunt Mag some more."

"Oh no," Edna said, "there's nothing to talk about."

"Shut the door behind you, girls," Aunt Mag called out heartily. "Just give it a good bang."

Edna did.

The Comeback

$\mathcal{W}$HAT HURT ERNIE THE most was going back to Mort and Ede. After all those letters he had written from the Coast talking about the big money, then to come crawling back to Long Island to sponge off of Mort's fifty bucks a week! On the other hand, why the hell not? Ede was his own sister and he'd done a lot for her when she was in school. That graduation dress he got for her one time, for instance; and how about the special price he got for the wedding party? It was the dough you put out when you only made a little that showed where your heart was, if Mort only knew it. But, oh no, all Mort could remember was the three hundred Ernie refused to loan him for his mortgage.

"Sorry about the mortgage coming due," was what Ernie had written Ede that time from Santa Monica. "I always said Mort wasn't ready to buy a house yet, and it seems I was right. Personally, I'm putting away every penny of my own in safe investments and recommending my clients to do the same."

So now every time Ernie asked him for a few bucks for expenses, Mort had to keep making cracks about those safe investments.

Ede was all right, though; no complaint there. She didn't say a thing the day he blew in from the Coast just in time for Sunday dinner. She moved the kid into her and Mort's room and let her brother have the nursery. It was kinda little and stuffy, but it wasn't bad once you got used to waking up to those blue ducks on the wallpaper. The kid was being brought up all wrong, selfish and spoiled, so naturally she put in a lot of bawling about wanting her room back, but you could get used to that, too. Ede said she'd get over it. Ede said she certainly thought it was wonderful that a boy like Ernie, who was never good at arithmetic, could have gotten all those big stars out in Hollywood to let him handle their money. Sure, she remembered how smart he was at P.S. 193—except in arithmetic—and how he nearly went to law school, but even so it seemed mighty wonderful. About then Mort would have to sound off.

"Have you been in touch with Clark today, Ernie?" he would crack. "I hope Bette and Tyrone haven't been pestering you calling up long-distance for financial advice. Maybe we better put the phone by your bed like you had to have it in Hollywood."

One night he hardly got in the door before he said, "By the way, Ede, I better warn you, Bing Crosby's in town and that means Ernie will be moving into the Waldorf-Astoria so he can take charge of his business details."

"O.K., blunthead," Ernie said coldly. "I'm a liar, then. I never was in Hollywood. I never had my own offices. I never been anyplace but right here on little old Long Island. Sure, oh sure, if that makes you feel any better."

"Uncle Ernie, did you really truly know Mickey Rooney?" piped up the kid. The kid was seven, with a fresh Irish puss just like Mort's and sprouts of sandy hair and a couple teeth missing.

"That's right, how about having Mickey out for a weekend

now you're here?" said Mort. "Honey would enjoy that, wouldn't you, baby?"

"Break it up, will you?" Ernie growled. "I got important things on my mind without listening to a lot of humor."

Even with Mort gone all day, the place was bad enough. It wasn't near the shore and it wasn't near the station. It was just the kind of house you would have expected Mort to pick out. Ede was one of those fussy housekeepers, too, always cleaning and washing, sloshing mops around under your new white shoes, making you move from one sofa to the next while she dusted it, and waking you up any old hour with the vacuum cleaner. Or else it would be the kid screaming for a dime for candy or Popsicles.

"If you gave her a nickel or dime, so much every day soon as she woke up, she might keep her trap shut the rest of the day," Ernie tried to tell them, but Mort just snapped back that if Ernie would try moving himself outa the porch swing once in a while, he wouldn't have to hear her.

Then there was only one car in the family, which Mort kept under his thumb.

"I'd like to get into New York once in a while, make some contacts," Ernie complained to Ede. "Sitting out here in the woods, I might just as well be dead."

"You could take a train, Ernie," said Ede.

"Train! I should start taking trains!" he said bitterly, for after all the lectures he used to give Mort and Ede on the handling of money, he couldn't very well admit that the bus fare from Los Angeles to New York had cleaned him out of his own two years' wise investments.

"I'd be worried about you, Ernie, with business conditions the way they are," said Ede. "But what I say to Mort is that anybody who could figure a job for himself in Hollywood the way you did don't need anybody worrying about them."

"That's right," said Ernie.

Looking back on it, he couldn't really hand himself much for thinking up his job in Hollywood. It wasn't even a new kind of job, but he had hardly been in the place a month before he knew the line he oughta follow. At every party his pal Hartley took him to, he looked for those babies in the money to shake a few century bills out of their pockets, but, oh no!

"Would you mind paying for these hot dogs, Ernie?" they would cry. "I haven't a penny. My business manager only allows me fifty dollars a week spending money and I won't have another cent till Wednesday."

"Fifty dollars a week!" another would exclaim scornfully. "He can't be much good if he lets you waste all that. Mine only lets me have two-fifty a day."

The envious way all the four-figure earners would stare at the clever one who had the most stingy business manager!

"I simply begged Hartley for a dachshund," another would boast. "I adore them, but Hartley just said another dog wasn't on the budget."

It wasn't long after that Ernie had horned into the business-managing business, and he was good, no doubt about it, or he couldn't have shoved Hartley out. There was hardly a day he didn't have some big name crying in his office for some little thing—a new necktie or a polo pony.

"Sorry," Ernie would say firmly. "We got to retrench. If I let you run over your allowance, then my other boys and girls would expect to, and it wouldn't be right. You're paying me to protect your future. Now, if you'll excuse me, I'll take a long-distance from my New York bank. I'm thinking of a new annuity for you."

At that, they loved it.

"Look!" they would run out and say to the next person they saw. "See these tears in my eye? But Ernie said no! Ernie knows best, you know. I understand he's considering buying me a ranch someplace, but he won't commit himself. Say, you ought to have Ernie handle you! He won't let you have anything at all; you don't have to give it a thought."

In a way it was a treat to see them hanging around his office after he'd collected the paychecks, waiting for him to dole out a few dollars spending money, to jack them up if they'd been gambling, give them the horse laugh if they thought they rated a new car or boat.

"Not on the budget," he would bark grimly. "Forget it."

The more he nixed, the better they liked it. They bragged of their defeats. He knew they had their little ways of getting around him, running up bills here and there, and saying, every time they sneaked in a few items not on the budget, "Ernie will kill me for this!" It was funny to see their faces when he caught them at the night spots throwing a big party he had refused them. He would drop a hand on the host's shoulder.

"O.K., Bart," he might say genially. "I won't say anything about this. Have your good time. But remember, the new piano has to be canceled till next quarter!"

It got to be a game how tight he could sew up their money so they couldn't outsmart him by borrowing too much. Maybe getting things sewed up too tight was what threw him out finally, or maybe it was because they couldn't get it through their heads that losing money on investments was plain business and not the same as throwing it away on a good time. Anyway, he was lucky the thing didn't get out, lucky there was no real scandal, lucky to be here on the Island with Ede dusting him off every five minutes and Mort making his snotty remarks.

"Listen, Mort," Ernie said finally. "A year ago I wouldn't let any little two-thousand-a-week pipsqueak talk up to me like that, let alone a fifty-bucker like you."

Even with Ede sticking up for him in her weak way, it was tough having nobody to listen to him when he explained market conditions. He would lie in the porch swing Sunday mornings, nothing on but his old beach robe, wiggling his toes, scratching his chest, smoking Mort's cigarettes, and discussing the financial news—that is, till Mort would start.

"Maybe in one of those checkered coats and suede shoes you sounded different," said Mort. "Maybe out in Hollywood they even listened to you in that dirty bathrobe. But me, I don't take financial talk from anybody unless they got all their clothes on, including a stiff collar and a cigar."

What could you do? You couldn't even tell a dumb bunny like Mort that it wasn't because you were a crook that you got through with Hollywood. Mort seemed to think there must have been something shady in handling thousands one day and then having nothing; it was a good thing he didn't know about that widow who started the row because Ernie had sewed up her husband's dough so tight nobody could find it. Mort, not being professional, couldn't take the long view.

The fact was Mort had only a fifty-dollar brain anyway, but a fifty-dollar brain can get you down just as much as a thousand-dollar one. "It isn't that I mind what Mort says," Ernie complained to Ede one day. "It's the way he gets my ego down. Once a guy's ego is down, he can't do a thing. Mort doesn't realize."

For the first time Ede seemed edgy. She was mending some silk underwear Ernie had asked her to fix up for him. (One good break, he still had his wardrobe.)

"Take Honey to the beach and forget about Mort," she burst out. "Here's a dime for her to stop her yelling. I got so much to do, Ernie—for God's sake, if you would just do one thing!"

It made Ernie kinda sore.

"O.K. I'm a nursemaid," he said. "All right, Come on, peanut."

Two years with his own suite of offices on Vine Street and now his flesh-and-blood sister had to ask him to air her brat as if he was a Polish nursemaid! He yanked Honey the half-mile to the beach and got her so out of breath she couldn't even bawl.

"My own sister! What a nerve! What a nerve!" He was still spluttering with rage when they reached the beach, and he lay on the sand scowling up at the sun and planning fine revenges while Honey paddled in the waves with a little boy named Edmund.

"Can I have my Popsicle now?" she squealed. "Can I have my Popsicle now, Uncle Ernie?"

"Pipe down," he said grimly.

"Mamma gave you a dime for me," Honey protested. "I want my Popsicle."

"You run back in the water," he ordered. "Maybe Uncle Ernie'll let you have a Popsicle and maybe he won't."

"Aw, Uncle Ernie!"

She splashed around reluctantly some more, and he could hear her fighting with Edmund and every other minute yelling, "Now, Uncle Ernie? Now?" Sometimes he would not answer and sometimes he'd just roar "No!" So Honey trudged woefully back and forth along the waves' fringe, tears streaming down her face. "Edmund's spending his dime!" she cried frantically. "Edmund's got his already!"

After a while, Ernie relented. He strolled over to the stand and bought a couple of cones. Honey and Edmund watched him eagerly while he leisurely bit into one and handed the other to Honey.

"Only I like Popsicles best, Uncle Ernie."

"You take what your Uncle Ernie gives you," Ernie said. "Uncle Ernie knows best."

"Yes, Uncle Ernie," Honey tearfully gasped. "Can I have my other dime now for a Coke? You got another dime for me, Uncle Ernie."

"Never you mind about who's got what," rebuked Ernie. "I've let you have your cone—that's plenty for one day. Now scram. Uncle Ernie's thinking."

"But—" quavered Honey.

"I'm in charge here. Scram!"

He lay back on the sand, feeling relaxed. Honey withdrew, sniveling over her cone, with tears and cream dribbling down her bare little chest. She kept her reproachful eyes fastened on Uncle Ernie, and the little boy Edmund, with ice-cream cone in one hand and Coca-Cola bottle in the other, stood beside her silently. They gazed at the recumbent uncle and then Honey saw Edmund's Coca-Cola.

"My Uncle Ernie won't let me have any Coke," she said with wan pride. "My Uncle Ernie only lets me have a cone. My Uncle Ernie knows best."

Edmund's pleasure in his own Coca-Cola was dampened. He withdrew the bottle from his lips and looked doubtfully from it to Ernie.

"I wish I had an uncle like that," he murmured wistfully.

They stood, licking their ices, staring fixedly at him.

"He won't let me have anything."

Ernie could feel their respectful eyes, even with his arm thrown over his face. He felt better than he had in a long time.

Feet on the Ground

$\mathcal{A}$FTER THEY LEFT THE Biltmore Vinie got into
the habit of vanishing completely, and then after a few minutes
appearing double or triple like a television picture. Bert decided
not to say anything about it, but worked on it privately and
finally licked the problem by squinting. He could keep Vinie
right in front of him by squinting steadily at him and once or
twice when he blurred away, Bert, by just squinching his eyes
up tight, brought him swimming back through red and blue
electric lights and stars in a blue ceiling—at first a very small
Vinie, then bigger and bigger till there he was, hiccups, straw
hat, and all.

"Let's call up Eve," said Vinie.

They were leaning on the bar in the front room of the new
place. A short dark girl with slick black hair kept coming
through the serpentine-hung archway and urging them to join
the dancers in the back where the music was. Colored paper

strands fluttered and flowed over her as she stood there, rosy and smiling like that old sewing machine ad.

"We did call up Eve," said Bert. "You talked to her."

"Eve's all right," said Vinie. "Eve said, 'Vinie, so long as you're with Bert I don't worry. Bert's all right,' she said."

"Sure, Eve's all right, too," said Bert.

"'Bert's got his feet on the ground,' Eve says," said Vinie. "You're sure I talked to her—oh my God, Bert, I don't remember!"

Now he was off again. Say what you liked, Vinie was still crazy as a hoot-owl. They ought not to have let him out of that sanitarium, they ought to have kept him there. Eve wanted him out though. Eve loved him. She said she'd see that he took things easy for a while; just don't argue with him, the doctor had said, never contradict him. Bert said he knew how to handle him all right.

Bert slapped him on the shoulder now.

"Let's go back and watch the dance," he said. "Come on."

Vinie was six feet tall, a big hulk of a man. People thought Bert was bigger, though, because he carried himself like a big fellow, shoulders high, head thrust forward a little. No matter how tight he got Bert always remembered to carry himself well, and if he ever slumped he snapped right into position again when he heard some girl's voice say something like, "Look what a fine physique!" Fine physique, he muttered to himself now, as the floor began to ruffle up around him, fine physique, so they made the back room and landed in a booth. Vinie, of course, stumbled into the wrong one right on to some girl's lap.

"What's this?" she said. "Hey!"

"It's Prince Charming," said Vinie, sitting down right beside her. "And this is my friend Stinky. What are you drinking, baby?"

"Martini made with vodka," she said. "Taste."

Vinie put his arm around her and took the glass that way.

"Your friend here is pretty tight," the girl said to Bert. Fine-Physique-Bert slid into the seat opposite her. She was pretty as a picture, and jolly, too, because Vinie's passes didn't make her mad, she just wiggled out of his clutch and laughed. Vinie was very quiet now, staring at her hard, the way a man does sometimes get sobered up by seeing something he likes.

"You'd better go," she said, still laughing, but she looked at Vinie as if she thought he was worth looking at. "I got a big boyfriend outside in the bar."

"Bert'll look after him," said Vinie. "Go on, Bert, be a pal. I just found my dream girl."

Mustn't contradict. Mustn't argue. Bert walked into the bar, swinging his body from the waist like a prizefighter. Somebody was doing a rumba on the floor, a Cuban couple, and the orchestra was playing "Mama Inez" the way it did all last spring down in Havana. First there used to come the orchestra, a regular jazz orchestra, and then the *son*, six native players with the *maruccas*, the drums, the clavos and the lace shirties. This must be the *son*, now, and it made him want to go to Cuba again and watch Selinda dance at the Sans Souci in the moonlight, with the giant palms walking away into the tropic night like elephant legs, walking away into the jungle dusk. Maybe he and Vinie could make the trip down there this fall; he and Vinie always had fun, but not now with Vinie all shot to pieces. Eve wouldn't let him go far. She stayed wild about him. She said, "'Bert,' she said, 'I wouldn't trust him with anybody but you, but you know how to look after him, just don't let him drink, stick to beer, but don't let him think you're bossing him.'"

No wonder the girl in the back room was so friendly to Vinie, for her boyfriend at the bar was nothing to look at. Big flat dark face like a pancake with eyes, and short, thickset frame, looked like a thug. Bert stood up beside him and ordered a whiskey sour. He looked at the boyfriend's shirt because it was just like the one he almost got yesterday; it was in Finchley's window and it was six-fifty. The tie was the four-dollar one he had wanted, too.

"That's the best damn tie I've seen in New York, bar none," he said.

The boyfriend looked at him and then clapped his hand down on Bert's shoulder.

"Kid, do you want that tie?" he said. "Here you are," and with that he ripped it right out of his collar and tied it around Bert's neck on top of his blue one.

"Now say, you mustn't do that," protested Bert. "Listen here!"

The boyfriend waved aside his argument.

"You can stand us a round of drinks," he allowed. "I'm having a gin daisy. Here's my card."

He pulled some cards out of his pocket and he and Bert exchanged cards. He might not be as good looking as Vinie but he was a hell of a nice fellow, and the girl was a louse to pass him up for Vinie, particularly since Vinie was crazy as a loon and this man was all there.

"If you're ever in Philadelphia, look me up," said the boyfriend. "I know the places there. I like a guy that knows good clothes when he sees 'em, buddy. Take that lid of yours. I'll bet you don't get a hat like that for less than twenty bucks."

"Take the damn thing," said Bert. "It's yours."

He jammed it on the boyfriend's head. It was a little small but it didn't look bad; Bert tilted it forward a little for him and it looked pretty snappy or would have if the man had had on a tie.

"That looks great," cried the boyfriend, watching himself in the bar mirror. "But look here you ought not to give me your hat. By golly, that's decent of you, old man. Say, what's your name?"

They exchanged cards.

"If you're ever in the vicinity of the Lombardy," said Bert, "I wish you'd look me up, I'd be tickled to death."

They had another gin daisy, then the boyfriend asked Bert to go back and meet his girl.

Vinie was kidding the girl when they got to the booth and she was laughing. When she laughed a dimple popped out at the side of her mouth and Vinie kept putting his forefinger in it and saying: "Whoa there, your face is running away." She was a creamy-white blond, but soft and warm looking, not like most of the Broadway blonds you ran into. Eve wasn't quite blonde or brunette, Eve—Bert thought of Eve sharply. Eve was all right, she was crazy about Vinie, she stuck to him through all the breakdown and the talk and the trouble, but Eve's funny little mug wasn't a thought a man could hold in the face of a lovely creature like this.

"This is my buddy," said Bert. "One of the swellest guys in this town."

"I'm mighty glad to meet you," said the boyfriend to Vinie, then he turned to the girl. "I want to say right here and now, honey, this fellow here is one of the few white men I've run across in my lifetime. We've only known each other half an hour but by God we understand each other." He shook hands with Vinie. "Here, have my card."

They all exchanged cards. The boyfriend happened to be the only one who had any cards so they all said Mr. William Stacey Woods. Vinie kept looking at his card before he put it in his pocket, and suddenly he put his hands up to his head and he was off again, the way Bert might have known he would be.

"Oh God, oh God," he moaned. "I don't even know my own name."

Then he disappeared and this time the boyfriend and the girl went too and Bert squinted his eyes hard till they floated back. Fine physique, he said, fine physique, he shouted, and right away he was all right again, but the girl just sat laughing at him.

"You're crazy," she said. "What's your name, anyway?"

"Woods," said Bert. He shouldn't have had the gin daisies on top of the whiskey sours, any fool would have known it. In a place like this he should have had a Daiquiri or a Bacardi or say a nice bottle of Marques de Rescal. That was the trouble with Americans. They came into a country like this to get away from home and all they wanted was ham and eggs or ice-cream sodas, that's why the Americans weren't good travelers and ought to stay home. There was something cosmopolitan in him, though, something a touch Spanish that made him fall for Mexico and the West Indies, particularly Havana.

"Have you been in Havana long?" he asked the short dark William Stacey Woods with no tie, and everybody laughed, but the big hulking William Stacey Woods leaned on the table again and began to cry. He sat there blubbering away and the Woods with two ties was sorry he'd brought him ashore.

"Woods here is on the wagon," he whispered to the girl. "He gets screwy on two drinks but don't argue with him."

"You slay me," giggled the girl and the dimples flashed like stars all over her face, and she was the prettiest thing he ever saw in his life, quick too.

"It's just the way it happened before," sobbed the big hulking Woods. "First I got to drinking, then I couldn't remember my name or where I was, then I got to crying, then they made me go to the hospital, and took away my penknife and then Eve came—oh Eve, Eve, it's happening again."

"We'll have one more drink and then we'll all go up to the Commodore," said the boyfriend Woods.

"Let's go out to Sans Souci," said the Woods with two ties. "We don't have to go back to ship till morning."

"The man slays me!" laughed the girl and leaned her head on the big crying Woods's shoulder. "Your friend is a scream. He thinks he's on a cruise."

Gin daisies fluttered through the air and settled down in front of them, but the crying Woods and the girl were making love and the two other Woodses stared at them, till the one with no tie and the too-small hat suddenly shot an arm out and socked the loving crying Woods on the nose, and the place was full of waiters.

"Don't be uneasy," said the Woods with two ties. "In Miami it's a lot worse, for there the gangsters do all the shooting, here it's the revolution, and it's better to be shot by a revolutionist than by a gangster, only you Americans can't see that."

The drums beat out a rumba and he could see again the tall palm trees walking away through the dark like elephant legs, and the thin high voice sang "Mama Inez"—*todos los negros tomamos café*—

"All the blacks drink coffee," he said, but he felt himself going, and he said fine physique, but he was still going, and Vinie had vanished again. He squinched his eyes and squinched them but Vinie would not come back.

Cheerio

*H*E WAS SURPRISED TO FIND that her apartment was so splendid. He was always impressed by venetian blinds and polar bears on floors, but aside from these wonders there were doors and corridors through which one could glimpse fabulous other chambers beyond. He wondered what her husband did. At the party he had not been very pleased with her. It was only after the more celebrated guests had snubbed him that he talked to her at all. She had seemed to him plain and far too noisy.

She came back into the room with a handsome bottle of Scotch under her arm and a couple of highball glasses. Undoubtedly her bracelet was real diamonds and whereas for many years such things had filled him with bitterness, tonight, since he was more or less a part of this wealth, he felt gratified. He had not minded his clothes at the party since the only other man who dared to be in tweeds was a Vanderbilt. He suspected that the Vanderbilt tweeds were a little stronger in the seat, however, and not quite as loose-woven as his own had become.

When she showed him her birthday present, the little gold pipe organ at the end of the hall, he smiled benevolently. It was flattering to be mistaken for a connoisseur of such luxuries instead of a man infuriated at sight of them. He relaxed in his fine chair, beaming at her, delicately sipping his highball instead of wolfing it as they'd been doing all evening.

"This is rally quat nahs," he said, rather surprised at the new deep resonance of his voice as well as the sudden British accent.

"Oh yahs," said Mrs. Parsons, catching it from him. "Well, here's how."

"When one has been working away in one's little cell as I have these many yahs, it's quat nahs to come out again in the sun," he said. "I must ask you to have a spot of tea with me sometime in my funny little place. It's in the Spanish quarter, you know, off Upper Fifth. It would amuse you no end."

"Oh, it sounds terribly amusing," said Mrs. Parsons.

"Of course I can't play for you. I had to let the piano go as you heard me telling Vaughn. Vaughn knew me yahs ago in Paris, when I was going to be the great concert pianist." He laughed indulgently. He wished he could get out of his unexpected English accent but it stuck like a burr, and he observed with growing concern that it had grown on Mrs. Parsons, too. He couldn't imagine why.

"Why don't you come here and play on my piano?" she urged him. "I'd love it."

He laughed again and he was pleased with the silvery quality of his laugh. He could have sat and listened to it all night, so delicate and charming and cynical it was. He couldn't imagine where he picked it up.

"You're too good," he said, "too good to me, entahly, Mrs. Parsons. As a matter of fact I've been thinking for some time of staging a comeback. My last concert was in, let me see, 1920, but I've kept up. A few pupils. Until of course I had to let the piano go. Now I write a bit—enough to keep me in tea and toast."

They both laughed at this and Mrs. Parsons's laugh had become almost as charming as his own. They sounded well together, the deep silvery chimes of his baritone and the delicate tinkle of hers.

"Why not have a little concert here, Mr. Falls," she suggested. "Let me give it to you. Please. Say about fifty or sixty guests, a little champagne and sandwiches. Please, Mr. Falls. Do let me."

He considered a watercolor on the wall thoughtfully.

"Picasso, isn't it? Ah yes. Segonzac of course. To tell you the truth, Mrs. Parsons, I think a small intimate concert would be exactly the way to open the season for me. A few important guests—"

"Listen here," said Mrs. Parsons, "I know some of the biggest people in New York. People that could make you, Mr. Falls. What's your first name?"

"Beachcroft," he said.

"Yes sir, Beachcroft," pursued Mrs. Parsons, obviously a little disappointed that the first name was in no sense an icebreaker but rather gave an added formality to the discussion, "I'd have fifty—no a hundred of the biggest people in New York here, all personal friends of mine, and they could make you, seriously. A word from them and you'd be made, made all over again I mean, Beachcroft."

"Oh Mrs. Parsons, you're too good, you're going to spoil me," he protested happily. "I might even get hold of Stokowski, a few musical figures, and of course I know Fink very well, personally."

"Fink is dead," said Mrs. Parsons, "I think he died in 1926."

"So Fink is dead," he said somberly, "I hadn't heard that."

Then he began laughing again.

"I was thinking of the champagne," he explained. "You don't

know how funny it is. If you could see my funny little place, rally literally, no bigger than that rug—"

"No, Beachcroft, not really! Ha ha ha."

"—and my funny little stove, and measuring out my coffee so carefully because coffee costs money, Mrs. Parsons, eighty cents a pound! And my ragged little tablecloth and my little French clay dishes with my black beans! I make a very good dish the second day of black beans. Add a spoonful of rice, a penny's worth of leeks, a bone—and here's the trick, Mrs. Parsons. I get my bones free at the market. I tell them I have a dog. Can you imagine me with a dog? Ha ha ha."

"Ha ha ha," laughed Mrs. Parsons. "That's delicious, too delicious. Getting bones for a dog you don't have."

"I've had him for years. And a very thoroughbred dog, too, Mrs. Parsons, a French sheep dog. He even has a name. Tiddley-winks. I say to the butcher, 'Please, Mr. Butcher, couldn't I have that nice little bit there for Tiddleywinks?' Rally!"

Tears of merriment were streaming down both their faces.

"Oh, Beachcroft you're killing me," gasped Mrs. Parsons. "Tiddleywinks. What a name for a dog that doesn't exist. Honestly. You're not joking?"

"I give you my word. I can tell you Tiddleywinks has saved my life many a day. I go out very little—the only person I keep up with is my friend Vaughn—but when I do I always beg a scrap for Tiddleywinks? Isn't it priceless? Isn't it perfect?"

"I've never laughed so hard in my life," sighed Mrs. Parsons. "But now about the recital we're going to have. I'm so excited about it."

"I'll begin with my Bach," he mused, examining his hands critically, "and then the Waldstine Sonata—or let me see—"

"Let's make it buffet instead of tea," said Mrs. Parsons. "And let's make a hundred people instead of fifty, or two hundred."

"Now, now, dear lady, you mustn't be too impulsive." He

wagged a finger at her and was a little alarmed to find he could not make it stop wagging. "A tea party, a little champagne, a little program—that's all that's necessary. I'll have to practice but perhaps Vaughn will loan me his piano—"

"Practice here," said Mrs. Parsons, waving her glass. "All day. Any day. I love it."

"Now for the guest list... hmm. I can't think of anyone but Vaughn at the moment, I've been so out of touch," he said thoughtfully. "I used to know a very good violinist once, very good indeed. He might play a group."

"Wonderful," said Mrs. Parsons. "Wonderful."

"I'd like to do something for him anyway," said Beachcroft. "He gave me a perfectly good hat once. Then he had some bad luck. I haven't seen him for eight years."

"Here's how," said Mrs. Parsons. She was sitting with her fat legs crossed under her and drinking with her eyes closed.

"You look like Alice in Wonderland, Mrs. Parsons," he said.

He began telling her about his violinist chum and times when they had shared their last crust together, but always gay, always delightful. When Mrs. Parsons drowsily mumbled that she loved bohemian life, he said it was wonderful to look back on but the trouble was he'd never been able to do so. They both laughed musically over this, though Mrs. Parsons's laughter was the weaker. She flattered him by little cries of approval at everything he said until he noticed with interest that she had perfected a way of conversing and sleeping at the same time. She snored but came out with a gentle "Uh-huh" at the end of each snore that sounded quite plausible and the height of good listening. He coughed. A clock struck surprisingly few strokes somewhere in the apartment. With a sigh he got to his feet.

"Well, this has been nahs, rally nahs," he exclaimed heartily, but Mrs. Parsons merely answered "Uh-huh" and went on snoring, her round little face tipped over to one side and resting on the jeweled left hand. "You've rally spoiled me, Mrs. Parsons, I mean it, literally. Now about the recital shall I call or will you—"

He waited a few minutes for her to speak. He picked a cigarette out of the bowl, looking around uneasily to see if he was watched, but after all in houses like Mrs. Parsons's they didn't care how many cigarettes you took. He took two. In the hall he managed to get into his coat, lining and all, and then he called out brightly, "Well, good-bye, Mrs. Parsons. Cheerio."

"Ssszzrrrr—uh-huh," said Mrs. Parsons. "Szzzzrrrrr—uh-huh."

In the street he realized that in taking Mrs. Parsons home he had spent his last cent. A walk would freshen him up, though, and he could plan the recital. For several blocks he felt very happy about it.

Artist's Life

$\mathcal{E}$VEN WITH HIS PICTURE in all the papers and his name on billboards over the theater not one of his old acquaintances could believe that it was really true.

"I always had a flair for the theater," the young author told reporters modestly, as he poured champagne for them in his luxurious quarters overlooking Central Park. "I studied all sorts of people in all walks of life with the theater in mind. It always seemed sort of second nature to me."

"You'd think he worked here once just to study us," Miss Hunter, secretary to the partners of the Elk Printing Company, observed on reading this interview, "instead of to earn his living just like anybody else. He makes me tired."

The only thing that reconciled her to his rise in fame was that at least it freed the office of his presence. She could hear herself think now, she told the other girls, and she knew the partners, Mr. Lewis and Mr. Frack, felt the same as she did. They could be themselves now. Chester had always made them nervous. Around the offices as he'd gone on his rounds filling ink bottles, emptying wastebaskets, he had had an intolerable habit of whistling operatic airs, fixing his bright knowing blue eyes on little Miss Hunter the while until she would have to look up from her work.

"*Tosca,*" he would laconically explain and resume whistling.

Sometimes Mr. Lewis and Mr. Frack would, in the height of a business argument, be suddenly paralyzed to catch sight of Chester right beside them, riveted to the spot, gazing at them, mouth agape, head cocked to one side like a reflective rooster eyeing a dogfight. At their indignant look he would resume chewing his gum and move on with his file basket. Was he studying them, they wondered later?

In his boardinghouse on Bushwick Avenue he was forever singing, richly rolling his fine empty baritone notes on snatches of songs with no words other than his improvised "*Cha manana da da dee machacaha — oh puchochoco dee dah myah love —*" He sang during his bath while the roomers waited their turn outside, holding their toothbrushes and bath towels and listening to all the hot water running away. He sang in great good spirits when he got up in the morning at six-fifteen. He sang on the slightest provocation. If you asked him a simple question he merely stared at you and then went into an outburst of music. He sat at meals without saying a word, his bulging blue eyes fixed unwinkingly on whoever spoke, his head twisted to one side like a ventriloquist's dummy. Suddenly—right there at table—his eye fixed on you, his mouth would open and a burst of song emerge—"*Oh cha dee chachacha — dee-dah — mucho —*" Then without removing his glassy gaze, he would stuff a roll in his mouth and munch slowly. Once when Ethel, the landlady's not too plain daughter, was passing his room—it was the little one at the end of the second floor hall that used to be her father's when he was alive—she glanced at him curiously for he was standing in front of the mirror, absolutely engrossed in his own image. He was not embarrassed at being observed but went into a new pose, chin on hand, three fingers upholding his cheek like a Pirie McDonald Thoughtful Tycoon.

"You know, Ethel, I may take up acting one of these days," he said thoughtfully. "Look, who do I remind you of?"

Ethel knew he wanted her to say Maurice Evans but she was bound she would not so she just shook her head and started on. He seemed a bit dashed and urged her to come in.

"I want to show you something," he said. He pointed to a grisly white clay thing hanging over his head. "Death mask of Beethoven."

Ethel looked and nodded feebly. He followed her to the head of the stairs and she was uncomfortably conscious of his unwinking stare following her all the way down.

The man's an absolute nut, she thought, irritated beyond measure, and then was startled by a fresh burst of operatic yodeling behind her, sudden and deafening, then absolute silence. An absolute nut.

After that she noticed that whenever possible he would seat himself in front of a mirror and watch himself as carefully as he had formerly watched other people. He would place an arm stiffly around another boarder's shoulder and cock his head to see how this looked in the mirror. All of his movements seemed carefully posed for a picture to be taken and he was forever glancing over your shoulder at the mirror behind you, not exactly preening himself, but with a detached scientific pleasure in the portrait presented. Ethel pointed this out to her mother but Mrs. Dalton merely replied that if she let little things like that get on her nerves she would have gone crazy long ago what with the Captain always spitting and Mrs. Boregarde talking Southern and Smitty putting sugar on ice cream. She reminded her daughter, a little heartlessly Ethel felt, that Ethel herself tried her hair ten different ways before the mirror every time she got ready for a date.

One day Chester brought a notebook to the table and while he ate he wrote busily with a very large brand-new fountain pen. He did this at every dinner after that and while people sat around the parlor talking after dinner. Sometimes he'd stop and smile absently at the others or read what he'd written to himself with obvious satisfaction.

"What in the world are you doing?" Mrs. Boregarde asked with concealed annoyance, for he had stared at her all that evening between pen scratchings.

"I am writing down everything people say," he answered frankly. "I am going to be a writer."

Everyone was silent for a long time after that, glowering at him—Smitty the garage mechanic who worked somewhere in Bay Ridge, Mrs. Boregarde's father, the old sea captain who chewed tobacco so there had to be cuspidors all over the house and was by his language forever giving the lie to his daughter's Alabama accent, Mrs. Boregarde herself who was having her face lifted by a long painless and invisible process so that she was always a different complexion but the girls at the Telephone Company where she worked pretended not to notice, and Ethel who'd been helping her mother ever since she graduated from High, two years ago. No one said a word, they merely glared at Chet until he finally closed his notebook, scrutinized the company with a bold penetrating eye, deposited the handsome pen in his vest pocket, and stood up. He bared his teeth in one of his rare and rather alarming smiles, for his expressionless face was like a window dummy's and a smile gave it a ghastly unreality, then he strode in measured steps out of the room.

"I never!" observed Mrs. Boregarde indignantly.

Her father wiped off his heavy walrus mustache with a red handkerchief and shook his finger at his daughter.

"Took down every word you said, he did," he cackled accusingly at her as if it was all her fault, "every goddamn word. Yes sir. Every goddamn word."

"I'm sure I didn't say anything, Dad," Mrs. Boregarde answered sulkily. "Nothing for me to worry about."

"Every time you opened that trap of yours," said the Captain with rising wrath. "Don't try to lie out of it neither, missy."

"Oh, Dad!" Mrs. Boregarde said wearily and went back to her *Screen* magazine. The Captain scowled at her all evening and muttered deprecations aloud until Smitty, who was working out a chess game all by himself, jumped up and yelled "Jesus Christ!" and went out, slamming the door behind him.

Ethel spoke to her mother about Chet's notebook, for he was never without it from that time on and meals were fraught with the most deadly silences. If anyone opened his mouth Chet's hand went to his pencil-pocket and out came the green fountain pen, attentive, waiting for the next word. Presently it was as Ethel said, like a house for the deaf and dumb.

"Well, what can I do about it?" said Mrs. Dalton, spreading out her worn, thin hands in a gesture of resignation. "He pays his board. It would be different if it was a typewriter and kept people awake. Or a baby. Or a saxophone."

Ethel took a look at the notebook one day, dusting his room while he was at the office. She saw:

CAPTAIN:	Pass the ham.
MRS. BOREGARDE:	Now, Dad.
CAPTAIN:	Ham, I said, daggone. Hey there.
SMITTY:	I don't know as it's any colder than yestiddy. Down to ten above yestiddy. Fella come into garage from upstate with snow on his car. Ten above, he says.
ETHEL:	Oh! Oh gee. That reminds me.

CAPTAIN: My daughter thinks ham's bad for me. Let me tell you I et ham forty years land and sea and I ain't dead yet.

MRS. BOREGARDE: Maybe somebody else might like some.

ETHEL: I forgot to mail your letter, Smitty.

CAPTAIN: Forty, no sir, by gad, forty-two years, land and sea and I ain't dead yet by a long shot.

ETHEL: I was in such a hurry to get home with the potatoes so I walked right past the post office.

SMITTY: Oh for Chrissake. Why'nt you tie a ring around your finger?

Dumbbell, Ethel thought, closing the notebook. The darned fool. Bad enough to have to listen to that day in day out without putting it all down in a book.

When she got dressed to go to the sorority on Valentine's Day she suddenly caught sight of him watching her through the half-open door. He was smoking a pipe as he had been doing lately, she suspected because he liked all the fine gestures connected with it, the unrolling of the tobacco pouch, the cleaning, the tapping, the big he-man drawing on it, the half-shut eyes as he inhaled, the reflective survey of the world through its billowing smoke. There he stood, big as you please, out in the hall, one elbow on the linen bureau, the other hand clutching his pipe bowl and calmly watching her get into her clothes. She was wearing the blue velvet dress she'd gotten at the shop Mrs. Boregarde had recommended down on Division Street in the city, and she had just had a permanent, $6.75. She wanted to look pretty because the girls always judged how popular or successful you were by your looks. She wouldn't want them to get the idea she was staying home because she couldn't get a job with all of her shorthand and because no one had asked to marry her for all her pretty face. She was fastening on her galoshes, sitting on the bed, when she heard Chet cough and realized he'd been staring at her all the time from the hall.

"You've got a nerve," she said.

He pumped away at his pipe without answering, then tapped it on the bureau top.

"Are you at all interested in sex?" he asked her.

"No," Ethel said.

She held her head very high as she marched down the hall, perfectly furious with him. She knew he was right behind her, watching the way she walked, counting the crystal buttons on the back of her dress, sniffing at her birthday-present perfume. She knew it and was not going to give him the satisfaction of turning around but since he was so quiet she couldn't resist just to see what he was up to. He was standing at the head of the stairs, meditatively.

"I am," he said. "Very, as a matter of fact."

At the office Miss Hunter reported him for using her typewriter every minute she was out of the room. Every time she came in from lunch there he was at her desk typing away with two fingers.

"Just a minute, Miss Hunter," he'd say in the most patronizing tone imaginable, and she'd have to let important letters wait while he pondered over a word, munching a cheese sandwich as he brooded. Usually he'd leave his trash mixed up in her nicely filed letters, so to teach him a lesson she threw half a dozen of his pages in the wastebasket. She smiled grimly as she heard him singing a few minutes later, all unknowing, bearing his opus to the incinerator.

"*Cha bla dee mucha busha*," he warbled. "Ever hear Flagstad, Miss Hunter?"

"I did not," she answered crisply.

"You missed something," he said. In ten minutes he was back, the crumpled pages in his hand. He held them out to her accusingly.

"Look here, Miss Hunter. What's the idea? That's my big scene."

"Nuts," she said coldly, and bent over her typewriter. She tried to ignore his reproachful blue eyes all day, until finally he offered her a stick of Spearmint to show he had forgiven her.

"You know something, Miss Hunter, you remind me of my mother," he said graciously. "Something about the eyes. I was just four years old when she died. Just a kid. You know, Miss Hunter, a kid without a mother doesn't have much of a chance in this world, isn't that so?"

"I guess you had plenty of uncles and aunts," she remarked, unrelenting, remembering that some uncle or other had gotten him the job with Lewis and Frack. But when she left the office he was sitting at her desk, chin in hand, ineffably sad and solemn, and she knew he was thinking that he was just a kid in a big city without a mother.

About this time he began growing a Van Dyke and the two partners in the firm fumed about the outrage of having a bearded office boy.

"When customers see him round the place they think we've gone into receivership," complained Mr. Frack. "You can't have an office boy looking like a banker—nobody'll trust us anymore."

At the boardinghouse the other boarders would not refer to it but the old captain never took his morose eyes off it from soup to prunes. Catching his eye Chester occasionally fondled the luxuriant growth, twisting the ends delicately above his somewhat sensual mouth.

"Anything to make himself conspicuous," Ethel said in disgust. "He'll be dyeing it next."

He took to excusing himself early from dinner and going up to his room. At the dining-room door he always lingered, waiting to be asked what in the world he was so busy about, but no one would ever do him the favor of asking. Finally he gave up his mysterious airs and sat around with the others in the living room after dinners, rattling a big typewritten manuscript, penciling in here and there.

Once in a while he'd leave it on the reading table right next to Mrs. Boregarde's *Screen* magazine and Smitty's *Radio Guide,* but no one would give him the satisfaction of examining it. He had to ask Ethel one night outright if she'd care to look at the play he'd just written.

"o.k.," she said, not too amicably.

So she read it with Chester watching her steadily, puffing away at his pipe. He couldn't have been more than twenty-two or three—she didn't see how he managed to raise that fantastic beard.

"You're skipping," he accused as she flipped through the pages. She only gave him a withering look. At the end she tossed it across the table to him.

"Well?" he asked complacently.

"I think it's terrible," she said sincerely and briefly.

He was not at all displeased but twisted the ends of his beard and laughed with great patronizing enjoyment.

"I knew you'd say that," he said. "Ho ho ho! I can read you like a book."

She heard him upstairs in a little while, singing in the bathtub: *"Che mucho dee dah dee muchoo di dee amorichimo—"*

"He isn't even bright," said Mrs. Boregarde. "I'll bet he couldn't pass the sixth grade. How can a dumb guy like that be a writer? I thought writers were supposed to have brains."

"Pooh," said the Captain, spitting across the room—he could almost make a curve out the front door into the street, Ethel thought—"I seen plenty writers. They got no more sense than a big-tailed bird."

"Dad," said Mrs. Boregarde. "Now, Dad."

Then the picture came out in the *News of the Theatre* one day. Chet passed it around at the breakfast table. Himself with a beard, leaning on his hand, bright eye fixed brilliantly on the reader. Smitty passed it silently on to the Captain who passed it on to his daughter. No one said anything. When it came back to Chet he took out his pocket knife and cut it out carefully.

"Yes," he said as if answering a question no one had asked. "Lots of money in the theater, if you have a flair for it. I got a flair for it. This fellow—my producer, understand—he tells me I've got the theater eye. I shouldn't be surprised if I quit work and took to plays entirely."

"Pass the jam," said the Captain.

Chester examined the clipping again lovingly.

"Chester Milton Cahill," he repeated and beamed at the glum faces around him. "I guess that gives you folks a thrill, eh? Got a big playwright living right here in the same house. May not be for long. I got my eye on a penthouse on Central Park West."

"That theater eye," said Smitty coldly. "Maybe you'll let us come see you sometime, big shot."

"Sure. Come up anytime," said Chet. He spotted Ethel backing through the pantry swinging door, coffeepot in one hand, a plate of toast in the other.

"Got to be off to rehearsal, now," he said. "Don't forget, Ethel, you're coming to my show. I'll see that you get tickets. Don't worry about that."

When she did not answer he pushed his chair back, pocketed his clipping carefully, stood up, and surveyed the group with head cocked to one side. His lips pursed into a piercing whistle as he strolled out. He paused to tap Mrs. Boregarde on the shoulder.

"*Aida,*" he informed her and continued out of the room, whistling.

"The darn fool," said Ethel.

"I'd like to bet on that play of his," said Smitty. "I'll bet it's a little honey."

"I don't believe a word of it," said Mrs. Boregarde.

The Captain wiped crumbs off his mustache and glared at the doorway.

"No more sense than a big-tailed bird," he muttered, and spilled jam all over himself like the old nuisance he was.

PART II

Audition

$\mathcal{I}$T WAS ELEVEN o'clock and still no sign of Danny. The two men waiting in Danny's apartment were struck with the same thought, simultaneously, and pushed aside the card table.

"He did it deliberately," Syd said. "'Be here at eight sharp,' he says. 'We'll get that second act set.' Then he never shows up. What kinda management is that? High-priced talent like us wasting time on gin rummy just because he don't show up. Unless he's got something up his sleeve."

"Whatever it is, it's no good," Eddie said gloomily.

There was a half-filled paper bag lying on the floor by the fire-place, with some empty pop bottles beside it. Eddie investigated the bag and found a couple of sandwiches left over from last night's conference. He offered half of one to Syd, who bit into it distrustfully.

"Liverwurst," he announced. "He always gets liverwurst. Ever since I said I didn't like it. Where do you suppose he went?"

He flung his sandwich into the electric logs of the fireplace.

"It's a cinch he didn't go anyplace that costs anything," said Eddie.

"Then he's gone back to his wife," decided Syd. "How much do you suppose he owes this hotel? Four hundred bucks didn't somebody say? Where's he gonna get that kinda money? Even if he finds a backer, how's a guy like Danny Bender gonna get his mitts on any personal cash? He ain't that smart."

"Boy, could I use money," mused Eddie. "I love money. Not for what it can buy, either. I love it just for itself."

He flopped on the davenport and lay back with his hands clasped behind his head, his feet crossed on the end table. Eddie was willing to admit that Danny's apartment was more comfortable for waiting than the little cubbyholes in the Ambrose on Forty-Second Street where he and Syd stayed. But he'd seen better places. Syd, however, never having worked in Hollywood like Eddie, thought Danny's suite was just about tops in luxury.

There were the gold-tasseled floor lamps, the glass coffee tables, the flowered plush davenport and easy chairs, the small Chinese red piano; and in the bedroom were the twin pink-ruffled beds, the window curtains of pink rayon, and the pink carpet. There was even a canary in a cage by the window.

"Some dame must have given it to him," said Syd. "Can you picture that louse with a canary? I notice it don't sing. Here. Here you are, bird."

He rescued a morsel of the discarded sandwich and poked it through the bars of the cage. The canary ignored it.

"All right, all right," Syd exclaimed angrily. "Wait for an order of caviar! A mug like Danny should have a bird!"

Eddie had a sudden thought and sat up.

"He's probably working on that crazy dame at the Plaza," he said. "If he thinks he can get money out of her, he should have his head examined. A woman calls him up on the telephone and says she's anxious to put money in a musical. So he believes he's got a backer. Never heard of her, mind you, never clapped an eye on her. 'Well, fellas,' he says when he hangs up, 'I guess our problems are over.' He don't even know a screwball."

"I'll bet he's there, at that," said Syd, shaking his head. "Sure, he's there. The old girl's probably got him locked in now, yelling for help."

The telephone rang. It was Eddie's turn to answer it. Already five girls had telephoned for Danny and it had been the two visitors' pleasure to inform them separately that Danny expected them at twelve. Sometimes the kids did show up and there was always a chance of a good time, unless Danny showed up too and got sore. This time it was no girl but Danny himself calling.

"You fellas still waiting?" he asked. He had his important, big-shot-on-Broadway manner so he must have been sure somebody was listening. "What about the revisions in that lighthouse scene? All set, eh? Fine. Did you catch that kid at Spivy's? No, no, not that one; she'll never see twenty-four again. I mean the one that just opened. Joan. They say she's terrific."

"Oh, sure, sure, Danny," Eddie said soothingly. "We signed up Jessel, too. No contract. Just outa friendship for you. Who's supposed to be paying for this good time we're having around town?"

"The Coast *did* call, then?" Danny asked urgently.

"Sure. Marie MacDonald telephoned up personally. Said she didn't want a lead, just a bit part for the honor of playing for you. She's on her way now on foot."

"I don't know whether we want MacDonald or not," Danny said crisply. "I'd sooner take a chance on Lake, even without a voice. We got a personality there we can build on. Look, Toots, punch up that lighthouse scene for me, will you, now? Get some gags, get Fats in on it. Remember this is four-forty not ten, twent and thirt."

Eddie made an insulting gesture toward the telephone and winked at Syd. Danny's voice was still going when Eddie spoke into the transmitter again.

"Listen, Buster, Syd and I have been waiting here four hours. Fats wants two bucks apiece for those gags he gave us or else he wants them back. No use calling him again. Where the hell are you? Have we got a show or haven't we? Are you coming back here and confer or aren't you?"

"Go easy, Eddie," whispered Syd, though he was smiling with admiration at his friend. "After all he's all we've got."

"Listen, Eddie." Now Danny's voice was lowered entreatingly. "Wait a minute, will you, fella? I'm onto something terrific. Will you take it easy now, till I get down?"

Syd was occupied with examining the correspondence in Danny's desk, and did not turn around until struck by his companion's silence. Eddie had hung up the receiver and was thoughtfully smoking a cigarette butt, selected with care from the ashtray.

"Crazy women do have money," he mused. "It just could be, you know. And if they'd go for anybody, they'd go for that George Raft type, like Danny. What's about that slick black hair, I wonder? It never fails."

Syd unconsciously began smoothing down his own sparse locks. He had taken vitamin pills for two weeks now to bring his hair back but so far nothing was happening. A songwriter could always get a girl, but even so, if you didn't have hair you had to have money. A hundred-dollar advance three months ago wasn't any nest egg.

"Let's call up the bar and charge some Scotch to Danny," he suggested. "If he's got the backer we owe ourselves a little celebration."

Eddie, for answer, silently dialed the telephone. After a while he gave up.

"Nothing happens," he said. "No outgoing calls."

"How we going to call up MacDonald and tell her we don't want her?" Syd acidly inquired. "She's probably got a hitch by this time. Shucks."

Eddie now seemed struck by an inspiration of great charm for he began humming significantly. He tiptoed over to the fireplace and as if by magic drew out a bottle of whiskey from beneath the logs. Syd shook his head again in awe of this mastermind.

"You did learn something in Hollywood," he sighed.

"You don't get kicked out of the best homes without learning something, sonny," Eddie said complacently. He fished two discarded paper cups from the wastebasket.

It was always a pleasure to put something over on Danny, so the drinks, which turned out to be a rather fiery Bourbon, were sipped with solemn appreciation. The phone rang again and this time, as Syd sprang to answer it, it was Carr, the agent.

"Where's Danny?" he shouted. "I'm in there punching every minute and he's got time to fool around. Do I shave? Do I have time to sit down to a meal at home? No, I'm on the hop every minute for that little fly-brain. Sixty-cent telegrams to the Coast every minute, a cable to London even, and when do I get my money back, do you think? Does Danny care? Do you two care? Oh, no."

"Why, Carr, you're talking like a man with an office," Syd cut in innocently. "Where are you—the drugstore?"

"All right, I got to do business from a drugstore because I handle dopes like Danny and that pal of yours, Eddie Rosman!" Carr snapped back ferociously. "At least I'm trying to do a service. I'm trying to warn Danny against that dame that calls up all the time from the Plaza. She's a screwball. Institution case. Stan just had a run-in with her, and she's bad. No dice there, so tell that clunk to watch out, will you? Tell him—the hell with it, there goes my nickel."

Syd put down the receiver and silently poured another drink. Eddie looked at him questioningly.

"Show's off—no backer," said Syd. "Now we celebrate that."

There was a knock at the door. Syd and Eddie, accustomed as they had become to angry landlords, summons servers, and other public enemies, looked at each other and with one accord hid their drinks.

"Nuts, they can't throw us out of a place we don't even live in," Eddie muttered. "What we got to worry about? Come in."

A little dark-haired girl, swathed in a long Persian lamb coat, stepped inside the door and looked hopefully at Eddie. They always looked at Eddie first because he still had his Hollywood clothes and that big chest, but they ended up with Syd because Eddie was too smart with them.

"You said I was to call at eleven," she said hesitantly. "About the show, I mean. My name is Miss Mink. Maribel Mink."

"How do you do, Miss Mink," said Eddie courteously rising. "I hope you won't think this is a joke but my friend's name here is Fink."

"Hey!" said Syd, annoyed.

Eddie raised a conciliatory hand.

"Just the first name. Now, Miss Mink, Mr. Fink and I want you to tell us exactly and in so many words just what you can do for our show. You dance of course?"

"Oh, yes," she said eagerly. Syd could tell by looking at her legs that she was no dancer, but they always said they could, and hoped God would hand out the gift like a little rain shower.

"When was your last New York show, Miss Mink?" Eddie pursued attentively, following Danny's auditioning manner so perfectly that Syd almost burst out laughing.

"Well, I'll tell you, Mr. Bender, I happen to have a prejudice against playing New York," the girl said earnestly, her large blue eyes moving from one to the other. "The way I feel is this, that a person gets a lot more experience in stock and on the road than they do in a New York show where a person is likely to get in a rut just playing one part night after night for a year or two, like a friend of mine in *Oklahoma!* I love the road, Mr. Bender, I really mean that. It seems crazy but I just never felt like playing in a New York show, I really never did."

Eddie stroked his chin. "Too bad," he said. "This is a New York show, you see, so you'd be out of luck."

The girl bit her lip. "I mean that's the way I *used* to feel, Mr. Bender. I wanted to be sure that I had enough experience to really make good on Broadway, and now I feel I really have, so here I am. I got looks—of course you're seeing me at my worst because I just got out of the hospital. I've been in the hospital for the past six months, and I don't look the same."

"What was it?" Syd asked, interested.

"They couldn't seem to find out," she laughed self-consciously. "All that money and all those doctors couldn't find out."

"What hospital? Sounds familiar," pressed Syd.

The girl gestured vaguely. "It was private," she said impressively. "You get better care."

"Do you sing, Miss Mink? But of course." Eddie took up Danny's role again. "Perhaps you'd sing something, ballad type, I should say."

"I couldn't without my own accompanist," Miss Mink said regretfully. "He's a Russian. Studied all over the world. Of course, he wants me to go into concert work."

"Naturally," approved Eddie. "And why not?"

Miss Mink was a little confused. "Because I got too many ideals, Mr. Bender," she confessed after a moment's thought.

"I like that spirit," said Eddie. "It's easy to see you're an ambitious girl. By the way, Mr. Fink, will you look at Miss Mink's profile for screen possibilities? You see, Miss Mink, we're thinking in terms of a package. We want to sell the cast along with the show to pictures."

"Oh, yes, a package," nodded Miss Mink, intelligently, and looked hopefully at Syd. Syd shrugged. She wasn't his type. He liked those tall blond clotheshorses from the model agencies. So did Eddie. So did everybody. That was the trouble.

"Nose a little broad," Syd said, offhand.

"It's my hair down," Miss Mink eagerly explained. "I can put it up. I wear it in a double pompadour created especially for me. I can't do it now, of course, because I don't have the pins."

"How old are you, dear? Nineteen?" asked Eddie.

"Almost," said Miss Mink. "Next Tuesday's my birthday."

She was probably twenty-three or four, or even older, Syd thought. That little dark kind fooled you.

"Fink, I think this is our girl," Eddie said, nodding wisely to Syd. Syd could tell he was kidding, and it didn't seem worth the trouble with this girl, so he gave Eddie an impatient signal. Sometimes Eddie made you sore, carrying things so far, but then Syd would remember that it was, after all, Eddie who once had the movie job and might get them both another one as a team, so it was better to string along with him.

"I'd like to know more about my part, please," Miss Mink said with dignity. "Naturally, I want to be sure it's right for me."

Syd watched Eddie go into a typical Danny routine.

"You're in and out most of the show," said Eddie briskly. "Your biggest comedy scene is laid in a lighthouse. You're stranded there with a Mae West character, a Bert Lahr character, a Betty Hutton, and say, a straight man, Tony Martin type. They start some crossfire, you give it right back, it's a howl; the West character gives you a sock line, voom and out. Lahr has a typical Lahr line, voom and out. Then three fast cracks, one right after the other, from Hutton, voom and out. Your juvenile looks at you—audience still howling, see—he gives you one terrific line, voom, and blackout. What do you say?"

Miss Mink pondered. "It sounds cute all right. Would I have to wear tights?"

"Certainly," Syd answered. "Say, do you live at the Artists' Hotel?"

"How did you know?" Miss Mink countered, startled.

"The coat," said Syd. "We've auditioned that coat a hundred times."

"I let the other girls borrow it," said Miss Mink, flushing.

"I knew you'd say that," said Syd. He was sorry for her, now, and he hated Eddie with his Hollywood past, and Danny with his elegant plush-and-pink apartment. Just because Miss Mink wasn't pretty like the other auditions, Eddie was taking her over the jumps.

"Supposing you sing us the hit song from this road show you speak of, Miss Mink," Eddie suggested, smiling.

"I'd love to Mr. Bender, I really would, but I've got this cold," Miss Mink responded brightly. "As a matter of fact that was what I was in the hospital for. Besides I work with a male quartet, mostly. They sang while I danced."

"Could you oblige with one of your routines?" Eddie begged politely.

Miss Mink frowned. "It seems sort of silly dancing without the male quartet after I was so used to it," she demurred.

"What outfit was it?" Syd asked, because he knew Eddie was going to.

"Oh, they've broken up, now," regretted Miss Mink. "The war."

"See here, Miss Mink," Eddie said quietly. "Would you mind telling me if you were ever on the stage in your life? You say you can't sing, you can't dance, I suppose you can't even talk, without that male quartet. Who do you think you're fooling?"

Miss Mink sat down quickly, as if her legs had given way, and her too large coat fell open, showing the shabby summer dress beneath. She began to cry, not prettily at all, but with snuffles and odd choking noises.

"You've got to get experience," she sniffled.

Eddie began to laugh, and this time Syd was really very angry. He went over and stood beside her, talking very fast and very loud.

"Never mind, Miss Mink, you belong. Don't worry about that. You're no actress, but that's all right. Eddie Rosman isn't Danny Bender, I'm not Fink, the backer hasn't any money, the phone doesn't work, the rent isn't paid, the canary doesn't sing, there isn't any show, and if there was it wouldn't be going on, and if it was Eddie and I wouldn't have anything to do with hiring talent, so what have you got to lose? Come on, now, I'll take you home."

Miss Mink rose weakly to her feet. "Why, that's sweet of you—" she said in a small tired voice. "Oh, that's awfully sweet."

Syd got his hat and coat, not looking at Eddie. Eddie sat very still, staring at the floor with a funny smile. He saw a whole cigarette under the fringe of the davenport and picked it up carefully.

"Come on," said Syd gruffly.

As Syd ushered Miss Mink out the door, he thought he heard a faint "yip." Syd didn't know whether it came from Eddie or the canary.

Such a Pretty Day

$\mathcal{A}$s soon as DAVE had put the pen in the yard and waved good-bye to the baby, Sylvia got on the phone.

"Hello, Barbs. Scotty gone, yet?... Listen, Barbs, Dave says they're working overtime this week so he won't be home for lunch... Scotty, too, eh?... That's what I wanted to know. Listen, Barbs, it's such a pretty day I thought we might go to the city. You bring the kids over and I'll get Frieda... Yes, I know she's a brat and she'll tell the whole neighborhood but she's good with the kids... Listen, don't say anything... My God, Dave'd kill me. You heard what he said last Sunday—if he caught me thumbing again he'd get a divorce? Listen, he means it. You come on over, Barbs. O.K. Barbs... Oh I'm goin' to wear my culottes... Your dirndl? Why don't you wear your culottes? They look kinda cute on you... Sew 'em up, why don't you? Or I will. Bring 'em over. Oh go on, Barbs, wear your culottes. I'm going to. O.K., Barbs. The baby's yelling. Don't forget the culottes. 'Bye."

Sylvia ran into the bedroom and whisked up the beds. She snatched up newspapers, toys, Dave's pajamas, a ten-cent double boiler with some petrified oatmeal in it and tossed them all in the closet. That was one thing about having your own house, your mother couldn't be nagging at you to do things her way all the time. Sylvia couldn't get over the thrill of her own house. Five whole rooms, just for her and Dave and the baby. Never had even one room to herself before she was married. Darn it all, she was happy. Let 'em talk. Her own mother was married at sixteen, too, wasn't she? Supposing she'd sat around and finished school, what then? She could have a job in the Lumber Works and get up every morning at six-thirty like Gladys Chalk, instead of lying around her own house all day in a nightgown. She could sit around waiting for some guy to call her up and God knows there weren't enough boys in town to go around, instead of having a nice fellow like Dave all sewed up permanently. So maybe Sylvia wasn't so dumb as her folks said. So what.

Mrs. Peters was out in the backyard fooling with the baby when Sylvia went out, and that was all right, because she could ask her about Frieda.

"You look about ten years old in those culottes," said Mrs. Peters. "I should think youda put on more weight being married two years already. I wouldn't take you for more'n twelve at the most."

"No cracks," said Sylvia coldly. "I was nineteen last Tuesday. Did you see the toaster Dave got me? We don't eat much toast but I have to keep at it 'cause it makes the baby laugh so the way the toast jumps out."

"I don't think that installment plan is good for young folks," said Mrs. Peters, as if it was any of her business, but Sylvia took it because she wanted Frieda.

"How else you going to get anything on thirty a week, Mrs. Peters?" she merely asked. "Look, Mrs. Peters, could Frieda come over today and look after Davie? I got a chance to go to the city—there's a picture I want to see at the Majestic."

Mrs. Peters blew out her cheeks and Davie laughed and squealed with joy. He was a good baby. Even Mrs. Peters had to say so.

"I couldn't run around the way you do when I was raising a family," said Mrs. Peters. "If it wasn't washing it was canning or berrying or helping in Mr. Peters's store."

All right, we'll go into that, then. The trouble with those old married women was they thought they had a racket all sewed up and they didn't like pretty young girls breaking into it.

"Tell Frieda she can make a cake if she wants too," Sylvia conceded. "There's flour and chocolate, and she can play the radio."

"If it's that Barbara friend of yours you're going with," said Mrs. Peters, "I wouldn't let any daughter of mine run around with her. Her folks are nothing but trash. There hasn't ever been a Moller that amounted to a stick in this town. Frieda says she saw six beer bottles in the sink there one morning."

"Barbs and Scotty are Dave's and my best friends," said Sylvia in her best Missus voice, and was that a lie, with Dave saying just what Mrs. Peters was saying all the time. "Tell Frieda to come about eleven, we want to get a good start."

Barbs walked in, wheeling the twins. They were not quite a year old but were big babies like Davie, and made Barbs look like a school kid, which she probably should have been, but keeping house was a lot more fun than figuring out "amo, amas, amat." You could say what you liked about Barbs, maybe she did run wild until Scotty and the twins kinda settled her, but you had to hand it to her she kept that dinky little apartment of hers spick and span. Sylvia didn't see how in heck she did it, but Barbs said she just liked scrubbing and washing and it was more fun than slamming through things the way Sylvia did. "Maybe," Sylvia always said, looking around the trim little suite over the butcher shop, "if I only had three rooms instead of a whole house I could get interested, too."

Frieda came over at ten minutes to eleven. She wore thick glasses over her slightly crossed eyes and her former pigtails had been miraculously transformed into a kinky tangled mass.

"I got a permanent," she said proudly.

Both Barbs and Sylvia were crazy for permanents so they were silent for a moment in envious awe.

"I don't like permanents on kids," said Barbs haughtily.

"Everybody in my Sunday school class has one," said Frieda, unperturbed. "My mother says it's a hundred percent improvement. My mother's making me culottes, too. Where you going, to the city? I thought Dave told you not to thumb anymore, Sylvia."

"Listen to the brat," said Barbs. "Do you run this town, Miss Wisie?"

"You better be careful or I won't take care of your old twins," said Frieda. "Can I really make a cake, Sylvia?"

Sylvia motioned Barbs into the house and they went in to whisper ways of getting out to the turnpike without Frieda being able to tell. Scotty didn't like Barbs hitching any more than Dave did, because everybody in the town talked enough anyway, and they said—they must have got together on this—Barbs and Sylvia were married women now and couldn't go coasting and hayriding and all the things they did when they were younger. At first Sylvia thought it was because Scotty was older—he was twenty-seven—and more settled, he'd worked in the factory since he was twelve, but then Dave, who was just twenty, got to talking that way, too. They didn't want their wives hiking around the state like a couple of tramps. You didn't see the Hull girls doing it, did you? Or Dody Crane?

"The Hull girls and Dody Crane, can you imagine," Sylvia repeated in indignation. "Why should they, they got their own cars, and Dody's dad is rich?"

At that Sylvia had nothing against Dody. The Hull girls were snobs because they'd gone away to boarding school while Sylvia and Barbs were plugging through public school, but Dody was all right, she always spoke to Sylvia, and once Dave had taken her to a dance. She wouldn't let him kiss her so he married Sylvia instead and promoted Dody to be his ideal. Sylvia got kind of sick of always being pecked at to do things the way Dody would do them. That was the only thing. But Dody was all right. She sent the baby a cute blanket once.

Barbs stuck the twins' bottles in the icebox and Frieda put all the babies in the pen. She was a fat little girl but that wasn't the only reason nobody loved her. She pulled out a camp stool from behind the tool shed and sat down on it on the grass with a book.

"I'll read to them for a while," she said, "from the Bible."

The three fat little babies, clad in nothing but their G strings, stared at Frieda, rather pleased with her glasses.

"They'll love that," said Sylvia, and she and Barbs sneaked out the front way, past the garage to the pike.

They walked sedately enough past the straggling houses, and tried not to look up at tempting cars shooting past, because you couldn't tell yet, it might be somebody from the factory who would tell the boys. A roadster with two men in it slowed up and one of them yelled, "Hi, Dietrich," but the girls dared not look up yet.

"You know, Sylvia, you do look kinda like Marlene Dietrich," said Barbs, studying Sylvia critically. "Somebody else, I forget who, said so. Me, I'm more the Merle Oberon type."

"You got freckles, too, if that's what you mean," said Sylvia, and then a No Trespassing sign on a fence reminded her of something and she giggled. "Remember Barbs, when the whole freshmen class came out here and stole apples one Saturday? No, I guess you'd quit school then."

"I was working in the Candy Kitchen," said Barbs. "I was going with that baseball player, Tod Messersmidt. Gee, Scotty used to rave. He'd just started boarding at Mom's. But gee, I was just a kid, going on thirteen, twenty-two seemed old to me, then."

A blue sedan drove slowly past, and Barbs nudged Sylvia. It was the Hull sisters on their way to the Country Club. They stared at the two girls and Barbs and Sylvia stared insolently back. Then Dody Crane's car came along, Dody driving with her mother, two golf bags sticking out of the side. Dody nodded and Sylvia nodded back.

"Dody was along that time out here," said Sylvia. "Her mother never let her come again because she heard there was necking. Ha!"

"I'll bet it's the last necking she ever saw," said Barbs, who after all had been ignored by Dody. "Imagine a girl that old running around all the time with her old lady."

"We used to have some fun in school," said Sylvia. "You should have stayed in, Barbs. I know I quit too soon, but I had two and a half years of high—that's about enough, most people say. You get the best of it. I suppose if I'd stayed till I graduated I would be riding over to the Country Club to play golf right now instead of hitchhiking with you."

"You would not," said Barbs drily. "You'd be helping out in the hotel kitchen just like your mother."

Now they were past the club road and on the main highway. They stopped and began working. It never took them long, because they were a couple of good-looking girls, as they well knew, and even women weren't afraid of being held up by such a nice little pair. This time it was a woman in a big Cadillac. She was a thin, browned woman with iron-gray hair and she drove like a house afire. Some fun. They were in the heart of the city in less than an hour.

"Let's go to the show right away," suggested Sylvia.

Everybody looked at the two bareheaded girls in their red culottes wandering through the business section. Barbs stopped short suddenly.

"Listen, Sylvia, I only got forty cents."

"But I told you we would go to the Majestic," said Sylvia, annoyed. "You know it's fifty."

"Well, I just don't have it," said Barbs, doggedly. "I guess you wouldn't have it either, if you had two kids instead of one and your husband had to fork over six bucks a week to his mother."

"Why don't she get on relief?" complained Sylvia. "Dave's mother did."

"Dave's mother is in another town," said Barbs. "And anyway Scotty don't like the idea. So I only got forty cents."

Sylvia was furious.

"I go to work and get Frieda for us and let her mess up my kitchen baking a cake, and now you don't have fifty cents for a show. Barbs, honestly, you're a lousy sport. Why didn't you tell me?"

Barbs was sullen.

"I wanted to get outa town for five minutes, show or no show."

Sylvia counted her money. Sixty-seven cents.

"You go alone, and I'll look around the stores," said Barbs.

It ended with them buying a Popsicle at a corner stand for lunch and then going on a shopping tour. They went through Schwab's because Barbs dared Sylvia to go in. This was a large, cool, dark, swank store and so snooty that Barbs and Sylvia clutched each other's hands to keep up their courage before the hostile clerks.

"This is where Dody gets all her clothes," said Sylvia. "Except the ones she gets in New York."

"A lot of good it does her," said Barbs, "I'll bet she'd give her eyeteeth to be married and have kids like we have. She played with dolls longer than any of us. She had the first mama doll in town."

"I wish I had a little girl," said Sylvia, "I'd get her a mama doll."

"I'd get her a Dydee doll," said Barbs, and that reminded her they must go to the Variety Store next.

Schwab's doors swung thankfully behind them.

"Even if I had money I wouldn't buy clothes in that lousy store," said Barbs. "Their styles are all hick. They've got braid on everything. Look!"

A window display of garden furniture, complete with sand, pool, umbrellas, and mint juleps held them spellbound. Life-sized velvety-lashed ladies in garden frocks sat in swings and deck chairs in attitudes of rigid enjoyment. A rosy wall-eyed athlete in shorts relaxed on a tennis roller. Two beaming little boys in bathing suits sat stiffly on a rubber dolphin in the pool.

"I could get the twins bathing suits and one of those false fish," said Barbs. "You know where I'd put it, don't you?"

Sylvia was thinking in terms of Davie but was willing to listen.

"I'd put it in the old tank on the roof and then fill it with water."

"Like a penthouse," said Sylvia.

They walked on silently to the big Variety Store, Sylvia busy putting the fish and Davie in a bathing suit somewhere around her own premises, and Barbs thinking about the tank. The Variety Store was more hospitable than Schwab's. A radio was on, and a girl at the piano counter in a pink sharkskin sport dress was playing and singing "If You Were the Only Girl."

"Say, if I couldn't sing better than that," muttered Barbs.

"It's my favorite song, too," said Sylvia. "But don't she ruin it?"

They hummed it softly, looking over the counters.

"I'll bet we could sing over the radio if we practiced more," said Sylvia. "Honestly, Barbs, even Dave thinks we're good."

"Ah, nuts," said Barbs. "Nobody's going to let us do anything ever. Wish I had my hands on that six bucks we sent off to Scotty's mom right now."

"I could let you have ten cents, maybe, if you want to buy something," said Sylvia relenting, but just then her eye caught something and she added, "Still, you got forty of your own, haven't you?"

Barbs saw what Sylvia saw. It was a baby's bathing suit for sixty-five cents. Probably it was only fair. After all Sylvia did have sixty-seven cents and only one baby.

"Now you only got two cents," was all Barbs said when the girl gave Sylvia the package. Sylvia unwrapped it right away and held it up. It was bright red with a little white belt. It was the cutest thing.

"I'd rather have had the striped ones like the ones in the window," said Barbs, but Sylvia read the envy in her voice and grinned.

At the next counter were spades and beach pails, and here Barbs was as lost as Sylvia because she had to buy two or nothing, so forty cents was no good. At the foot of the counter were rubber floats and one was a dolphin almost like the one in the window. It was a dollar ninety-eight and it came in a box, then you blew it up. Sylvia and Barbs stared at it.

"Kids don't need bathing suits on a roof," said Barbs. "I can fill that old tank anyway."

"Sure," said Sylvia.

"You can bring Davie up to play in it, too," said Barbs, generously. "But he won't need that suit."

"That'll be fun," said Sylvia. Sixty-five cents wasted.

They could not take their eyes off the sample dolphin.

"He'd hold two, wouldn't he?" said Barbs.

"Sure—three, even," giggled Sylvia.

She almost knew what Barbs was going to do and yet in a way you could have knocked her down with a feather. The minute the clerk walked off to the next counter Barbs had snitched one of the rubber things out of its box and stuffed it down her front. Nothing happened. Nobody screamed. Nobody grabbed them. Barbs looked at Sylvia, and Sylvia's mouth moved helplessly.

"W-w-w-well," said Barbs, "I g-g-g-uess we'd b-b-etter be g-g-g-going to the M-m-m-ajestic."

They walked slowly out of the store. A man in a Panama hat watched them from the record counter, but he couldn't be anything but a customer. The girl at the bathing-suit counter watched them.

"She saw," gasped Barbs. "Just as I popped it in I saw her looking, but it was too late to yank it out, then. Look.... I'm afraid to—is anybody following?"

Sylvia was afraid, too. They walked in slow agony down the street. Someone was behind them. Out of the corner of her eye Sylvia saw it was the man in the Panama hat. He grinned. Sylvia grew red. Barbs clutched her arm frantically.

"Let's get a hitch, quick," she whispered. "We got to go home now."

"But it's only two o'clock," said Sylvia. "Anyway if somebody's watching from the store they'll see us."

"Oh—oh, what'll we do," whispered Barbs. "Does it show?"

Sylvia giggled.

"No, you only look like Aunt Jemima, that's all."

Barbs was looking up and down the street for a possible hitch. The man in the Panama hat was getting into a Chevrolet coupé. He grinned again, and imperceptibly winked. Barbs and Sylvia walked up to him, but before they spoke two men in shirtsleeves from the Variety came out on the sidewalk and with one accord the girls climbed into his car. He slammed the door and drove quickly around the corner.

"Oh gee," breathed Barbs. "Oh thanks!"

The man was a swarthy foreign-looking fellow, with a candy-striped shirt and a diamond ring.

"I got the idea," he said.

Nobody said anything more till they were outside the city limits and then Sylvia noticed they were not going in the direction of Butterville.

"Pittsburgh's my next stop," said the driver. He turned to Barbs. "That wasn't your first job there in the store, was it, sugar?"

Barbs looked blank.

"Don't act so innocent," he said, laughing. "I knew what you girls were up to as soon as I saw those red culottes. But you'd better not work that store again. They've got you down, now. For that matter you'd better leave that town alone awhile."

"I don't know what you're talking about," said Sylvia, with dignity, "And anyway we're not going in this direction."

"What do you say going to Pittsburgh with me and then on to New York? A couple of girls like you could clean up a thousand dollars a week—just the big stores, understand, nice merchandise, not ordinary snatching. I could send you straight up to a friend of mine on One Hundred and Thirty-Fifth Street and you'd be treated right. A couple of nice kids like you could get away with murder. What do you want to waste your time stealing bathing suits and rubber gadgets?"

"I bought this bathing suit," said Sylvia angrily.

"Why—" gasped Barbs, "you don't think we're thieves?"

The girls looked at each other in growing horror at his sardonic laugh.

"Of course you're not thieves, honey," he chuckled. "You was just taking what you liked, that was all.... Don't kid me, sister, you're a smart girl, both of you, for that matter, you got talent, you could do big stuff, I'm telling you. I did you a favor today, why don't you do me a favor now and try out the big time? You could wire your folks."

"We're married women," said Sylvia. "Our husbands would come after us."

"Think it over," said the driver, good-humoredly. "Drop me a line, if you change your mind. You say you live in Butterville?"

Barbs and Sylvia exchanged a despairing look. Too late to get out of that.

"We're moving away from there, soon," said Sylvia.

"You might give me your names and I'll drop you a card, reminding you where to get in touch," said the man. He pulled a silver pencil out of his pocket and a card.

"Dody Crane, Butterville," said Sylvia.

"Teresa Hull, Butterville," quavered Barbs.

"Well, Dody and Terry, you'll hear from me," he said, and slowed up near a filling station. "You're the best talent I've seen in these parts. All you need is training and a little protection."

At the filling station he got out and went inside. Without a word Sylvia and Barbs slipped out and ran to the road, hiding in the bushes along the way. They saw him come back out and look for them briefly, question the mechanic, then with a shake of his head he got in and drove off. Barbs and Sylvia looked at each other and drew a great breath of relief.

"I never was so scared," said Barbs. "Believe me, I'll never swipe anything again."

"I should hope not," said Sylvia.

Barbs pulled the rubber out of her dress and began to blow it up. Sylvia watched. Barbs's face grew redder and redder and the fish grew bluer and bigger. It was bigger than the one in the window. It would easily seat the twins and Davie, all three. Then, Barbs's face grew worried; she took it away from her mouth.

"I forgot to take the darned stopper," she panted, and tears stood in her eyes. "Oh, darn! Oh Sylvia! Darn, darn, darn."

"Maybe a piece of paper—" suggested Sylvia, but the fish collapsed, dwindled to nothing. Barbs looked down at it in the middle of the ditch in disgust.

"I would forget the stopper," she said, "I'd have to forget the most important thing."

"Why didn't you tell me you were going to do it?" said Sylvia. "I could have helped you do it right. Honestly, Barbs, you may keep your house better than I do but you're dumb about lots of things."

This is the last I go with her, she thought, I didn't even get to see a picture.

An empty ice-truck drove along and Sylvia and Barbs jerked their thumbs in the Butterville direction. The car slowed down and they climbed in among the burlap bags in the back, where a young man in a bathing suit and dirty white slacks sat, fiddling with a harmonica. The girls settled themselves in the corner opposite him.

"I still got forty cents," Barbs said.

The car jolted them along the country roads, past cornfields and waving wheat.

"Hi, Dietrich!" the boy said to Sylvia.

The girls looked at each other and laughed.

"What's that you're chewing?" he asked.

"Bubble gum," said Sylvia, and snapped it.

He said nothing more but stared at them as he played his harmonica. Barbs and Sylvia sang while he played their favorite piece, "If You Were the Only Girl." they sang all the way going into Butterville. The boy and the truck driver both said they ought to be on the radio, or at the very least, the stage.

The Grand March

$\mathcal{V}$ELMA'S MOTHER SAW Mrs. Raymond come out
on the porch with her knitting bag, a sign that the boardinghouse
supper was over. She called softly from Velma's bedroom window.

"Want to watch Velma get ready now, Mrs. Raymond?"

It was the least they could do for her, Mrs. Clinton had told
Velma. The lonely old widow was obliged to make her living expenses by renting her tiny cottage to the Clintons and having no
one of her own, she was grateful for a small share in Velma. She
loved to sit with Mrs. Clinton and watch Velma get dressed for
parties—it was almost like going to a party herself. Velma was so
fussy, doing everything the latest magazines advised; making up
her face with a glossy foundation and no rouge, spraying perfume on her hem, adding a special touch to the simplest things.
Mrs. Raymond often declared that those society girls and even
Hollywood stars could learn something by watching Velma.
Now, at Mrs. Clinton's summons, she hurried across the cinder

driveway and came in the bedroom just as Velma had finished her bath and was getting into her underthings. Mrs. Clinton, with the fatal attraction of the overweight for small chairs, squeezed herself resolutely into the little boudoir chair and with a finger raised for silence, as if in a theater, motioned Mrs. Raymond to the pine rocker.

"Tonight's the annual banquet at the plant," Mrs. Clinton explained confidentially. "Velma's never missed one since she was twelve years old and started to work there. It's always a big affair. All the big shots from the office—even the Mayor—will be there."

Velma smiled at Mrs. Raymond. She wasn't exactly pretty, Mrs. Raymond admitted, but she had learned pretty little ways, and she was always friendly and good-natured.

"Everybody kept telling me today, 'Now, Velma, be sure not to miss the banquet tonight,'" Velma said, brushing her soft brown hair before the vanity mirror. "As if I ever missed one. I said, 'For heaven's sake, where else is there to go tonight in a town like this?'"

It was a pleasure to see how daintily Velma's dresses were hung away in their cellophane bags on ribboned hangers, little satin sachet bags tied to each one. You would think that a hard-working girl like that wouldn't have time for all that extra fuss, but even with office and home work Velma took time for all the fancy touches. Every article she was going to wear and every cosmetic she was going to use was carefully laid out before she even started dressing.

"I don't know where she gets it," her mother marveled. "Never traveled outside this state, never had rich friends to teach her."

"I can tell you one thing," said Mrs. Raymond. "Whether she ever traveled anywhere or not, there isn't another girl in town that has as much style or is as well thought of as Velma Clinton. And, as everybody will tell you, she's certainly earned it."

Velma made a laughing grimace at them in the mirror as she braided her hair.

"Hey, will you two stop talking about me while my back's turned? Or else tell me something I don't know."

"Full of the Old Nick," said her mother, fondly. Then she leaned forward, frowning. "Velma Clinton, you're not going to the banquet with your hair like that. Pigtails!"

"Oh, Mother, all the kids are doing it!" Velma winked at Mrs. Raymond and impudently tied a bow on the end of each braid. Her nail polish and lipstick were exactly the same shade, Mrs. Raymond noted with satisfaction. The new dress laid out on the bed was white, and the bag beside it was green patent leather like her sandals. Velma was a fashion show all by herself, Mrs. Raymond observed—and if all the younger crowd was wearing pigtails, then Velma could get away with it a lot better, because she had style.

"But Velma's thirty!" Mrs. Clinton demurred.

"Here we go again," Velma sighed to Mrs. Raymond.

"If everybody in this town didn't know each other's business, they wouldn't take her for over twenty." Mrs. Raymond stated. "Those pigtails make her look just like a kid. She'll get a lot of compliments."

"She always gets plenty of compliments. They spoil her there," said Velma's mother. "Go on and tell what that old boy at the plant said yesterday."

"'Miss Clinton, if you'll permit an old bachelor to say so,'" Velma obligingly imitated a deep masculine voice, "'had I seen any girl in my time who had your dash and go, I'd be a grandfather today,' It's Robert Marbe Jr., the personnel manager."

"Old enough to be her father, almost," Mrs. Clinton said. Both ladies chuckled with thorough enjoyment at the ridiculousness of the other sex in its later years.

"*Junior,*" Mrs. Clinton repeated scornfully. "It kills me. If I was able to get around, the first thing I'd do would be to give that old man a piece of my mind. He's got no right to pester a nice girl like Velma."

"I guess you think nobody's good enough for Velma," said Mrs. Raymond, smiling. "I know how you feel."

"I declare if I could afford it I'd take Velma right out of the plant on his account," Mrs. Clinton went on. "He's always after her to go with him to the Juke for dinner, or go to a show in Hillsdale. Why, Velma wouldn't dream of it!"

"He's got no one but himself to look after, why shouldn't he spend a little?" argued Mrs. Raymond.

"All right, but why can't he pick on someone his own age?" cried Mrs. Clinton, her round pink face getting redder with righteous anger.

"Never mind, Velma, you go ahead and get a good time out of it," recommended Mrs. Raymond. "Men are scarce enough nowadays."

"I'd never hear the last of it," Velma said. "Mother would razz the life out of me. So would the kids at the office. They're always kidding me about him. He's much older than the rest of us, see."

"I'll bet he's fifty if he's a day," said Mrs. Clinton.

"Still and all, it would be nice for you to go out with a fellow once in a while instead of always with the girls," Mrs. Raymond said, although she could see that Velma's mother was ready to explode with protestations.

"But Velma doesn't want to get mixed up with any fellows," she said. "She's funny that way. She's got her friends and her good job and her home just the way she likes it—I leave it all to her—and she doesn't want to be bothered with fellows."

"Sure, I have a good time," Velma agreed. "I get my raises regular. I got no kick."

Both ladies opened their eyes wide as Velma slipped into the short white dress that left her arms and back bare. Velma giggled. Sometimes she got things just to see her mother's and Mrs.

Raymond's eyes pop. It made her feel frivolous and fast, and that was a rather exciting feeling.

"It's a good thing it's mostly girls there tonight," said Mrs. Raymond. "My!"

"Why, I tell you these girls nowadays have more fun, just girls together, than our generation did with all our beaux," Mrs. Clinton declared. "Picnics, bridge parties, ball games night and day, sewing parties, bazaars, raffles, trips. Something doing every minute. Just girls, mind you."

Velma, in the midst of painting her lips with a small brush, paused to pout at her audience.

"I'll have to take a back seat by myself now that the fellows are coming back," she said. "No man of my own."

"Listen to her!" said her mother. "To tell the honest truth, there isn't a man in this town that Velma would give a second thought to. She's too particular, and she's got too many ideals. I guess her old mother kinda spoiled her, letting her have her way in every little thing."

Velma was thoughtfully studying her costume. Then, to the delight of her audience, she took a pink carnation from a glass on the vanity and pinned it on her shoulder.

"Who but Velma would think of that?" exclaimed Mrs. Raymond.

"That's what I say," Mrs. Clinton agreed. "Still, I don't know about pigtails. Even if I hadn't always been poorly, I can't imagine myself going out in pigtails and barefoot sandals at her age."

"I'm supposed to be on crutches, Mrs. Raymond," Velma laughed. "When I was first working at the plant, Mother wouldn't let me go places because I was too young, and now she says I'm too old. Honestly!"

"Never you mind," consoled Mrs. Raymond. "You keep young because you go with young folks."

"The kids at the plant don't think of her as older than they are," Mrs. Clinton admitted. "She's always the life of the party, fixing up suppers for them, making everybody have a good time. I tell her she does too much for those girls. It makes me sore sometimes when the couples pair off and go someplace without inviting Velma."

"That's not their fault, Mother," protested Velma. "I can't go to high-school alumnae parties when I never finished school, can I? I can't go to parent-teacher dances, can I?"

A horn tooted outside the window, and Velma ran to the window to peer at the car now coming up the driveway.

"Hi! Be right out!" she yelled.

The older women watched her fondly, appraising her swift graceful movements, the childish thinness of her body, the swing of her walk. Velma read their admiration and laughed self-consciously, tossing her braids over her shoulder.

"I'll bet Junior will have something to say about those pig-tails," Mrs. Clinton sighed, shaking her head disapprovingly. "It's just what he'd like, the old goat. Thank goodness, she has enough self-respect not to pay any attention to him."

They followed Velma to the door, certain that the friends in the car would exclaim over her appearance. When they heard the cries of "Doesn't she look darling?" and "Oh, Velma, you old sweetie!" they nodded to each other proudly.

Back in the tiny living room Mrs. Clinton, panting a good deal over the effort, got out the card table and chairs for their evening card game. Mrs. Raymond shuffled the cards. They sat without playing for a moment, thinking of Velma, and how hushed the house was without her fragrance and gaiety.

"She's never given you a minute's worry," mused Mrs. Raymond. "Most girls stuck in a little town like this would be off to the city to get a husband, leave you to shift for yourself, the way I've had to do."

"Velma thinks more of her old mother than most girls do of their husbands," Mrs. Clinton said. "She never forgets a birthday. There's always some little present when she comes home from her week at the lake with the girls. She's always fixing up the house, painting the furniture, tending to all the things a body in my condition can't do. Pitched right in working as soon as she was old enough after Mr. Clinton died. Always sees the bright side, never a cross word."

"And so stylish," said Mrs. Raymond. "Every little thing just so."

"Why, when Velma was only twelve and just an errand girl at the plant, she used to wear those little blue denim uniforms as if they were Paris models. Now me"—Mrs. Clinton cast a deprecatory glance at her own shapeless body in its baglike print housedress—"well, maybe I might have had the knack too, if so much sickness hadn't made me lose my figure. Velma's lucky she hasn't had to have a family."

The telephone rang and Mrs. Clinton waddled to the hall to answer it. The office manager wanted to know if Velma had started for the party yet. It seemed they had a surprise and wanted to be sure she was going to be there.

"That settles it," Mrs. Raymond said. "We'll just have to wait up to see what the surprise is."

Mrs. Clinton dealt. "They always think up some devilment," she said. "Last year they made Velma give a speech on why she broke her engagement to Charles Boyer."

"What time do you suppose the party'll break up?"

"She won't stay out all hours, I know that," Mrs. Clinton answered. "She knows I'll be sitting here worried. But not only that, she has more pleasure just talking things over with me afterward than she does at the party itself. She knows nobody appreciates her the way you and I do."

"And Junior—don't forget," Mrs. Raymond laughed.

"I wish he'd stop pestering her," said Mrs. Clinton, irritably.

"There's always somebody like that to take the joy out of life. Why can't he let her have a good time?"

It was barely eleven when they heard Velma's step on the sidewalk outside.

"Funny nobody drove her home," Mrs. Clinton pondered, listening.

Velma came in quietly, latching the door behind her. "You two night owls still up?" she asked.

"What's the matter? Didn't you have a good time?" asked her mother uneasily.

"Swell," said Velma shortly. "I just want to go to bed."

"What was the surprise?" eagerly asked Mrs. Raymond. "We've just been dying..."

Velma handed a small gold pin to her mother and slipped into the bedroom.

"Look what it says," cried out Mrs. Clinton. *"To Velma Clinton, oldest female employee of the Western Connecticut Hydraulic Works, for 18 years of faithful service.* C'mon, Velma, tell us all about it. Aren't you tickled?"

"The Mayor made a speech and so did the manager and I bowed and everybody cheered," she said in a tired voice. "Then the noise and everything made me feel sort of faint so I came home. For goodness' sake, can't I come home early once in a while?"

"How'd everybody like your pigtails?" Mrs. Raymond asked.

"Oh, fine," said Velma, though Mrs. Raymond noted her hair was now pinned in a bun on top of her head. "I went into the drawing room and pinned them up, though, after I got that Oldest Employee pin. I don't know—I felt silly."

"I was right then," exclaimed her mother, triumphantly.

"Oh sure, you're always right," Velma said, in such an odd tone that Mrs. Raymond, sensing trouble, hastily offered her a cup of coffee.

"All that excitement, no wonder you felt faint. Here, take this. Is it all over now?"

"There's the Grand March finale," Velma said, "I was to have led it with the oldest male employee—Bob."

"Bob?" repeated Mrs. Clinton. "You mean Junior? Well, no wonder you came rushing home to get out of that. I don't blame you."

"Oh, Mother," said Velma.

"That's real gold," Mrs. Raymond said, examining the pin. "Solid gold. That'll last you a lifetime."

"That's right," said Velma, with a dry laugh. "A lifetime is right."

"I don't care what anybody says, it shows that sticking to your job year in, year out—none of this flitting from place to place—is what pays in the end," Mrs. Clinton said.

The telephone rang and Mrs. Clinton, lifted eyebrows expressing her surprise at the late call, went out to answer it. She put her head back in the door presently, with a wink at Mrs. Raymond.

"It's Junior," she whispered. "He wanted to know what happened to Velma. He said"—here Mrs. Clinton gave her own exaggerated interpretation—"'Your daughter certainly looked pretty in those pigtails tonight.' Can you imagine a man his age—"

Suddenly Velma sprang to her feet, her eyes flashing.

"Will you please stop insulting my friends?" she demanded. Then, in a low, choked voice, she continued, "I don't see that there's anything funny in making jokes about a person's age. He's the only friend I've got—at the plant or here either. He's not nearly as old as you are, so what's so funny about him?"

She snatched the receiver from her mother's limp hand and the older women heard her change to a gay teasing tone.

"Hi, Bobby. What about the two faithful old employees doddering out to the Juke tomorrow for a private celebration? What do you say we play hooky for once? They think we're too old to work, anyway."

Mrs. Clinton's shocked, bewildered eyes sought Mrs. Raymond's for sympathy as her daughter's voice dropped to an intimate murmur they could not hear.

As she said to her many times later after Mrs. Raymond moved in with her, it wasn't that she minded Velma having a man of her own after all these years, it was her showing such disrespect for her old mother.

But Mrs. Raymond didn't say anything.

Here Today, Gone Tomorrow

ℐNCREASINGLY THE WORLD she had left became desirable. She began to write long letters to a few of those she remembered although she had never intended to do this. She had intended to float away mysteriously into this free air—New York, a room at the Hotel St. Albert—while back there they would constantly ask, "What *has* become of Miss Chilton? Doesn't anyone hear from her?" There was that essay of hers in the *Hibbert Journal* last winter, mute evidence of her success, but she was tired of imagining their gasps, she wanted to *hear* them. She wanted to hear the whisper the first week of school among the freshmen as she strode, lean, bareheaded, gaunt, across the campus, "That's Miss Chilton!" And the older girls would say, "Wait till you get her in History Seventeen! It's worth coming here four years just for that!"

She longed once more for those crisp October days when her sensible shoes crackled over forest paths and wheat stubble on her Saturday hikes while at the gate as she started off groups of eager-eyed girls would call, "How far will you walk today, Miss Chilton?" and she would twist her fine red mouth into a wry smile and her deep, decent, square-shooting voice would say, "Oh, about fifteen miles, I daresay." Their buzz would follow her. "Isn't she marvelous? Isn't she a perfect peach? Oh I do think she's *swell!*"

She missed the Sunday night supper talks in Fieldsley Hall with Miss Palmer—all the girls listening. Miss Palmer, fluffy-haired and bespectacled, was niece of the Archbishop Palmer, no less. How the freshmen gasped as she calmly argued her atheistic or non-Episcopal points, how Miss Palmer sputtered, flushed, gesticulated. "But surely, Miss Chilton, even if you don't believe in the Episcopal Church, you must believe in something, in some Infinite Good—perhaps some Force, something like Emerson—" All eyes on Miss Chilton, who would sit stirring her tea, fine gray eyes staring into the fire, stout woolen leg crossed over woolen knee. They waited, breathless, not daring to guess what new shocking thought would come from her.

"I believe," she said casually, "if anything, the Unitarians are as close to the real thing as we can come—in our time."

"Oh! Oh! Oh, but Miss Chilton! Surely, Miss Chilton!" No doubt that Miss Palmer was flouted, red-faced, and a little weepy, or rather not Miss Palmer but her uncle the Archbishop Palmer with whom Miss Chilton had been secretly arguing.

She missed the Dean's puzzled admiration. The Dean was a clever woman. She knew how brilliant Miss Chilton was, perhaps better than the others knew. And of course at commencement it all came out when Dr. Chilton, in beautifully variegated hood, took second place in the Academic Procession, usually carrying on a spirited talk with the silent bearded visiting speaker. All along the aisles the girls whispered, "She has three honorary de-grees, besides her Ph.D.—Yes, yes! yes! Isn't she marvelous?"

It was on these occasions after the commencement speech, as the faculty stood around the Dean's exquisite drawing room, many of them for the first time, it was then that the Dean's real admiration came out for her history teacher. "Doctor Beadel," she would say or Dr. Swithens or whichever famous educator the visitor happened to be, "be careful of Miss Chilton, here—she has very dangerous ideas of religion, I assure you! A very naughty girl, Doctor Beadel."

She would press Miss Chilton's arm laughingly and then, her academic robes billowing about her, would rustle off to the next group, leaving the excellent guest to bend toward Miss Chilton with well-bred interest. "Is this true, Miss Chilton? Well, well! I, myself, am not too convinced a Wesleyan. I often ask myself whether with all our Protestant creeds we have accomplished half as much as the Vatican. Seriously, Miss Chilton—"

She would not be unobservant of the Dean's interested glance as they talked, though no closer intimacy ever came between the Dean and herself. The former almost knowingly selected the day before vacation for her modest overtures so that no further advantage could be taken of them.

She missed the second day of the second semester when her supreme lecture was always delivered. She always wore the same thing for this lecture, a short green leather jacket into the pockets of which she thrust her strong brown hands, striding up and down before the class. Alumnae wrote to their younger sisters in History XVII—"I envy you the thrill of hearing Long John on Attila. My dear, you'll be too thrilled for words!" Miss Chilton knew the girls called her Long John and was secretly well pleased. She was always clumping down to the table and with a wry, boyish smile murmuring, "Don't know whether I can get all my legs under here or not—am I all over you, Miss Breen?"

Her lecture, "Attila, Savior of or Menace to Western Civilization," year after year brought the same breathless silence into the classroom. This was why they elected History xvii. This was why, in the catalogue, the Dean always referred to "our particularly strong History Department." She loved that awed hush before she began her Great Lecture (without notes); she loved playing with it, sitting down at her desk reading a letter with a casual dreamy smile as if unconscious of this great moment in everyone's life. The quiet, sardonic beginning as she turned her fine, clean profile to the window—"Attila was—like King Arthur—a scoundrel yet a boon to humanity."

The gasps—"Like *King Arthur,* Miss Chilton? You don't mean like *King Arthur!*"

Her calm reply, "Like King Arthur."

Always, after the lecture, pale students waited to question this and that point, to protest against the heresy that ran nonchalantly through this Perfect Lecture. With a quiet amused smile how brilliantly she parried their choked, indignant questions! After she was in bed that night there would always be some tormented little wretch to tap timidly on her door and whisper, "I want to talk over the lecture, Miss Chilton. It's upset me terribly. It's not at all what Robinson and Beard said, really!"

Here in New York, reflected Miss Chilton, she could say anything wherever she went and no one lifted an eyebrow—no gasping here over scholarly radicalism. Sitting here in the little dim-lit lobby of the Hotel St. Albert, just off Gramercy Park, sitting here as she had been every evening now for many months, thinking of the school, of Fieldsley Hall, of the Dean, Miss Palmer, and the rest, she was glad at least that it was she, not those poor innocents, who had to make the adjustments to this outside world. She had never been *of* the school, as they all were; she alone had been of the world. Ten—twelve—no, eighteen years in one room on one campus was not enough to confine her free spirit. Every third summer she had spent her month in Switzerland, for where but in Geneva should a history teacher be? Other summers were spent in the Canadian lake regions, or perhaps at Chautauqua. More than this, there was her long connection with the *New York Times*. It had followed her wherever she went; its bound volumes brightened her simple rooms; it was a faithful record of everything that had happened to her. In the school dining room or in the drawing room after dinner, no matter what the discussion, someone was sure to turn respectfully to her and say, "What does the *Times* say on that, Miss Chilton?" and she would graciously interpret the *Times*'s policy.

She remembered that autumn day, years ago, when her heart had missed a beat on seeing a fat Sunday *Times* being handed to one of the new girls at the mail desk. There was no reason, of course, why someone else shouldn't subscribe to the *Times,* doubtless any number of perfectly stupid people did, people with no appreciation of the dry wit, the scholarly allusions, the calm just grasp of world affairs. The *Times* was fair, naturally it could not discriminate in its subscribers, yet Miss Chilton could not help examining with disapproval this new person to whom the *Times* had so blindly intrusted its political secrets. This rival subscriber was a slight little blond girl of sixteen, with pretentious violet eyes and an elaborately red mouth. Instead of a flapping sport coat she wore a most inappropriate pale blue silk suit. Obviously she was not a subscriber of the *Times*'s own choice. Miss Chilton disliked her, was indeed forced to flunk her in History xvii, but publicly was forced to defer to her constantly. *And what does the Times feel about Wilson's new note, Miss Chilton?* "Naturally, the *Times* feels—and I quite agree—" Miss Chilton would patronizingly explain, but if little Shirley Bell was present she was forced to add, "Wasn't that what you gathered, Miss Bell?" One day, however, Miss Bell, drooping her pretty blue eyes, blushingly confessed that she never read the paper, that Uncle Bert sent it to her, but she was so ashamed, she never even looked at it! Miss Chilton, woman of the world that she was, continued to smile pleasantly at the child, but in her own fine, loyal breast there seethed such a wave of indignation and outrage that it was with difficulty she kept from writing to the *Times* himself (for she thought of the journal as a him, a suave, reserved, dignified man of fifty with a neat Van Dyke, a man in fact not unlike Dr. Beadel, president of Wilburt College for Men).

During the war the Dean frequently and graciously called upon Miss Chilton to talk in chapel, not only as head of the History Department but as the *New York Times*. In deference to the Dean, Miss Chilton wore her academic robes for these occasions, and wished that Dr. Beadel, or rather the *Times,* could hear her excellent summary of the world situation. His, or rather the *Times*'s face, as he wrote his now grave, now pungent editorials, must have worn much the same wry smile as Miss Chilton's did in quoting Him. "As the *Times* says—rather deliciously, I think—" she would preface the jest, though some of the undergraduates had learned by this time that anything referred to as "delicious" was never funny but it was always as well to smile decently or breathe ecstatic appreciation.

To add to the crime against the *Times* the freshman Shirley Bell was never present at these chapel talks. Passing through the Lower Dormitory one day Miss Chilton had seen the charwoman carrying a wastebasket full of unopened *Times* down the hall from the freshman's room. Eventually Miss Chilton was able to avenge this outrage, for the Dean called upon the history teacher personally, to chaperone the girl Shirley Bell home to Syracuse after she was expelled. It was no pleasant task. Shirley wept all the way home and once, Miss Chilton was positive, had sent a telegram to the *man* but Miss Chilton looked away, her clear eyes and well-chiseled mouth delicately registering her contempt. It was indeed a rather dreadful experience for Miss Chilton, as the Dean must have foreseen, occupying the same compartment with this girl who had disgraced the school so that the morning the scandal had broken, the dining room was as silent as if someone had died, and several of the girls were openly crying. Only Shirley Bell had brazenly giggled, drank her coffee with zest, and appeared not to notice the cold shoulders of the older girls. She had stayed out overnight, but worse, had confessed when rebuked that she had been secretly married for over three weeks! Miss Chilton was, in her sophisticated way, rather amused at the Dean's and other teachers' dismay, their horror that a married woman had actually been harbored unknown to them, for three whole weeks, in this sanctuary for decent girls, that while the school was going on in its pleasant, calm way as it had for a hundred years, respectable girls were being contaminated by this wanton. For days, even weeks afterward, the Dean had her meals served in her room; she could not face her flock lest she read some new and horrid knowledge in their young eyes. But it was Miss Chilton who had to spend the night on the train with the girl, and to hear her sobs all night, "But Miss Chilton, I love him! And there's nothing so terrible about getting married!"

"I believe it was the secrecy of it the Dean disliked," Miss Chilton had to say a dozen times. She looked steadfastly away as Shirley, with not the slightest shame, fussed about with no clothes on. Naturally the human body was a fine thing and Miss Chilton herself had the classical attitude toward it, but there was a slight difference, as she was sure the *Times* himself would have put it, between the human body and a newly married body. Impossible to ignore the faint decadence of a bride's body, accompanied as this one was by some wretched French perfume and gauzy underthings.

"And why can't I stay with Lester instead of being sent home this way to Uncle Bert? After all Lester *is* my husband? Miss Chilton, you do see that."

"Undoubtedly, my dear, but the Dean feels, in justice to her position, and since the marriage was made without her permission, you should be returned to your home and allow your uncle to judge the next step."

"Uncle Bert lets me do as I like," Shirley had wept. "I want to stay with Lester!"

The compartment reeked of perfume. Miss Chilton could only sleep by conjuring up the piny smell of the Canadian woods. And even now, years later, a chance whiff of that heavy jasmine recalled the slimy horror of that night.

Uncle Bert was at the Syracuse station, a fat red little man who merely patted the girl and said, "Why, where's the young man?" To Miss Chilton he had said, "You know Shirley's traveled all over the world alone—you needn't have come."

"The Dean thought a chaperone wiser under the circumstances," Miss Chilton had rather coldly responded. "Naturally, I had no wish to come."

"They thought I'd marry every man I saw on the way home," Shirley had bitterly observed. "They think I'm forming a habit so they have to be on guard."

Uncle Bert laughed and apologized to Miss Chilton for Shirley bothering the school, reiterated again that it was too bad the young man hadn't come along, he'd like to meet him—This, then, was the creature who had sent Shirley the *Times*.

"What were her people like?" asked the Dean, who was not at all a snob but felt that people were more easily handled when nicely placed in their proper category.

"Middle class," tersely answered Miss Chilton, and the disgrace was never mentioned again by either of the two women.

What if this affair had been handled by a less worldly member of the faculty, Miss Chilton often thought, little Miss Palmer, for instance, who cried over the girls' broken engagements, the alumnae's babies, and had a most naive grasp of sex? There was obviously not one woman of the world in that group of ten teachers in Fieldsley Hall. Not one really, thought Miss Chilton, whose life was not utterly confined to her little room. Think of it, she mused, twenty—thirty years within their little four walls! If she herself had spent nearly twenty years there at least she had never been buried, as they. Her room had the unmistakable mark of a citizen of the world—altar cloth from a Hindu temple over her fireplace, a framed Sangorski parchment, a pair of skis, a Russian samovar, an autographed photograph of an ex-ambassador to Japan (formerly a historian), iron miniatures of Bismarck and Napoleon, a Congo mask, a Samurai sword, books, books, and books. No pink ruffled provincial curtains here as in Miss Palmer's pretty but unquestionably limited room, no lace pillows, no pastel furniture, no investment to reveal plans for permanency as these other rooms did. Her room, with its continental-stamped trunk always open in the corner, showed how temporary her stay was here, each foreign bibelot showed the world-traveler, the nomad, the cosmopolite, here today, gone tomorrow. The Dean knew this. Each year for eighteen years at the Farewell Faculty Supper (farewell though most of them were to return in the fall) when each teacher told her plans for vacation, the Dean would bend her charmingly marceled gray head toward Miss Chilton. "I tremble to ask *your* plans, Miss Chilton," she would sigh, "what is it to be this year—China or Alaska—whichever it is, don't forget to come back to me in September."

Miss Chilton would laugh indulgently and after a rather good pause, say meditatively, "I'm rather tired of the Jungfrau. I think I may try the Dolomites. Let me see—it's been ten years since I've seen the Dolomites."

Once the assistant chemistry teacher, a silly creature who only lasted a year, had shyly inquired what a dolomite was—she'd heard so much about them.

"Don't you know your Swift?" Miss Chilton had drily countered and the Dean had burst into a peal of well-bred laughter.

"Oh, Miss Chilton, that's delicious! That's simply delicious! You *are* a naughty girl!"

Afterward Miss Chilton could not imagine how that exquisite *mot* had come to her, but like all inspirations she concluded it was useless to examine the source, merely be grateful for that moment of felicity, be grateful too that the Dean had been present to repeat it, later, with decently twinkling eye, on state occasions, and moreover to repeat it correctly.

Lately Miss Chilton had felt curiously let down about the Dean. She had written her—after waiting several months to whet curiosity as to what *had* become of Miss Chilton, she had written her amusing, blunt, characteristic letters with a few terse comments on the national economic situation in her old vein. In reply she had received a pleasant but impersonal dean-to-former-teacher note that was most flattering, though in perfect justice to the Dean, Miss Chilton saw that their intimacy, in fact their equality, had never been more than an understood relationship. In the *Alumnae Monthly* she read that the new history head, a Miss Hornickle with the merest M.A. polished off by a brief smell of the Sorbonne, had electrified the students of History XVII by her brilliant lecture on her particular subject—"Catherine the Great, Soviet Benefactor." No need to conjecture as to changes in the other departments. Almost every teacher had her one pet, as every actress has her favorite role; Miss Palmer's Juliet was "Influence Moral or Decadent of the Brook Farm Group," and each year both before and after this tremendous emotional climax Miss Palmer was to be found in her bedroom at Fieldsley Hall, shades drawn, her head swathed in icy cloths, bromides and other medicaments on the night table, and frequently the resolute little creature dissolved in tears.

Poor Miss Palmer, thought Miss Chilton, it would never have done for her to come out in the great open world; cloistered walls were no prison but a kind protection to such gentle souls. Even there she lived in a constant flutter of apprehension. She feared night, sleeping with her light turned on; she was afraid to pass the Village Hotel for strange men leered at her from its windows; she was in bed two days after their trips to the city to see *Dracula;* she had one year a complete nervous breakdown because of the new janitor who, she swore, peered in her bedroom with a telescope ingeniously directed from the Astronomy Room. She dared not fully undress for weeks, even with drawn shades, but covered behind a screen in her good woolen underwear and brown sateen slip, then flew across the room to bed, removing her clothing under the comforter though even then she felt that the magic eye of the janitor's telescope could bore through shades, blankets, even skin, like some demon X ray.

"Stuff!" Miss Chilton had told her with an indulgent laugh, swinging her long legs from the chair by Miss Palmer's bed. "What if he can see you—perhaps he looks at all of us—"

"He does, Miss Chilton! I'm sure he does!" earnestly exclaimed Miss Palmer, her blue eyes swimming in tears. "And every time I pass him on the campus—that horrible old man with his dyed mustache and depraved face—I could just die!"

"Stuff!" Miss Chilton had repeated. "I doubt if he peeps at any of us, and even so what's a human body more or less—even nude—"

"You don't understand!" moaned Miss Palmer, and buried her head in the pillow once again. "You wouldn't understand. Running all over those foreign countries has made you hard, Miss Chilton, it has, I may as well say so."

To placate her Miss Chilton had spoken to the Dean herself over a specially made pot of coffee in the Dean's private apartment, the Dean in a trailing gray velvet house gown for she had been dining alone in her rooms for weeks now because of migraine or secret state problems. As two women of the world they had smiled a little over naive Miss Palmer's apprehensions, but the Dean had instantly become serious.

"I'll see the man myself at once," she said, pulling the velvet bell cord she had always preferred to buttons. "One has to take precautions where nearly sixty girls are in one's charge. Senator Cudfly's two daughters, for instance—and the Van Sweet girls—"

"Of course," agreed Miss Chilton, for the Dean's glance had said that she and Miss Chilton alone understood these matters, they two were intrusted with these well-born charges, statesmen's daughters, millionaires' daughters, Dr. Beadel's niece, and a mass of lesser souls whose function was largely to provide tennis partners and companionship for their gilded sisters.

The new janitor had been a character. The Dean and Miss Chilton were obliged to laugh after his visit. Yes he had used the telescope, he admitted, because he liked to look through telescopes; for that matter he always looked through all the microscopes, too. It was a treat to see some of those things in a drop of water. He had asked the chemistry teacher what they were and she said, "Heliozoa." Had the Dean ever seen any heliozoa? She ought to go over to that laboratory some day and take and put a speck of ordinary water on a slide—As for peeping into the windows of Fieldsley Hall—"What would I be doing looking at them old girls?" he had sarcastically demanded. "I got an old woman of my own."

"Really quite a character," the Dean had laughed after he left.

"Merely trying to educate himself," said Miss Chilton, and again the Dean laughed. What would she do without Miss Chilton, she seemed to say, one person with whom she could share a cosmopolitan sense of humor.

Miss Palmer had to be sent away for a week's rest but was never quite herself till the man was discharged. Yes, Miss Palmer would have been horrified by New York. She had been saucereyed at the faculty supper when Miss Chilton had let fall her bombshell.

"And where *this* summer, Miss Chilton?" The Dean had asked her annual question. "East or West?"

Miss Chilton had toyed with her timbale of mushrooms and sweetbreads—one always had the best food at the Dean's table—and without looking up, had said nonchalantly, "Oh I'm staying in America, as a matter of fact I'm settling permanently in New York."

New York? Permanently? Not leaving the school—no, no—surely not that?

"Oh yes," Miss Chilton had pleasantly answered. "I don't like getting in a rut. After all I never intended to make a *career* of teaching."

"I knew you wouldn't stay with us," the Dean sighed in genuine dismay. "I felt it in my bones! I said so when you first came! I said—'Miss Chilton must be regarded as temporary—she will never be happy here for long.'"

"But what will you do?" Miss Palmer had gasped. "I don't mean to be rude, but how will you live? Really, Miss Chilton."

"I have saved a bit, naturally, then I intend to spend my time writing," said Miss Chilton in her composed crisp way. "Rest assured I shan't be idle."

Proof of her success was in the December *Hibbert Journal.* She was, moreover, working on an essay on "Attila: Myth, God or Man." She had, in her letter to Miss Palmer, referred to the satisfaction of creative work after her five—no eighteen—years of teaching. Miss Palmer had written back, stoutly declaring that for her part she felt molding young minds was just as creative as any other art. She added that New York might suit Miss Chilton but, although she herself had never been there, she was certain that she'd never be able to work in that clatter of night clubs, gang wars, and gambling. Fieldsley Hall had suited *her* for twelve years, it would suit her for as long as she lived. The ivy had been beautiful last year and the new botany teacher had made a rock garden for the Dean where in fair spring weather the Dean promised they might have tea. The new freshmen were a very nice lot; they had three connections with Cabinet officers, a ward of the Governor's, and two daughters of the great steel millionaire who were very sweet and not at all Jewish-looking. The Dean herself had commented on it.

Clatter of night clubs—how like Miss Palmer to picture that as New York! True, at this moment a well-modulated radio was pouring through the St. Albert lobby dance music from some night-club orchestra, a crooner's voice in fact was singing some ballad, "I'll Follow My Secret Heart."

Miss Chilton put down her magazine and with her hands in the pockets of her tweed jacket strode through the meager palms of the lobby to the desk. "Mail in?"

It was Tuesday and the *Alumnae Monthly* always came on Tuesday. The clerk looked nearsightedly over his double-lens glasses, saw the fine, brown, leathery outdoor face of Miss Chilton, her smooth gray hair drawn sleekly to the back of her head.

"Nothing, Miss Chilton."

The Dean hadn't written, Miss Palmer hadn't written, the two favorite graduates hadn't written, the *Alumnae Monthly* was late—frowning Miss Chilton went back to her chintz-covered chair by the reading lamp. This morning's *Times* lay on the table but she had already read it through and more and more it was receding from her life as she saw every day dozens of quite obviously stupid people buried in the *Times*. She picked it up now, idly, and adjusted her glasses to find some new treasure in it but the radio music crept through the pages, the silvery round tenor words floated sweetly through the Market Page: "I'll follow my secret heart—"

In an inexplicable way the voice was like a sweet, suffocating perfume, like heavy jasmine, like—yes—like Shirley Bell. It was all Miss Chilton could do to banish the suffocating sweetness from her thoughts, though she focused her mind firmly on the fine clean fragrance of the Canadian woods.

Deenie

The best thing about Walker was that you could always count on him to be on time. A nice change, Liza thought, from a man like Fletch who never showed up anywhere less than forty minutes late. When Walker said seven-thirty at the Swiss Pavilion, he meant he would be there at seven-thirty. None of that "whoever gets there first, hold a table" business, which meant that you sat there for hours, with waiters demanding, "Is Madam alone?" No, Walker would be there in person, with a corner table reserved—and better still, enough money for dinner and plenty more in his wallet.

Walker's wife could loiter through the arcade buying cunning trifles in the little shops, as Liza was doing now, comfortable in the knowledge that the money she had with her was hers to spend and that her man, when faced with the dinner check later, would not fumble through his pockets murmuring, "Good heavens, I seem to be short! Darling, do you happen to have a couple of fives on you?"

"A solvent man is like a melody," Liza was humming to herself in the Caribbean shop, when she heard a familiar voice behind her.

"Why Liza-Liza!" it said, thus identifying itself as part of her boarding-school past. Liza turned and recognized Deenie Bronk, with mingled emotions of remorse and pleasure. Excuses for unanswered notes, unacknowledged gifts, and phone calls rose to her lips. But it was too late, of course.

Deenie had been a big girl on the campus, Liza's roommate, and the one Gables girl with whom she had "kept up" when they both came to New York later. Deenie had won trophies for shot-put, high jump, long-distance running, and hockey at Old Gables, and she had the gaunt, prematurely gray appearance such dissipations often give. She wore her good tweeds and her good bombproof felt as if they'd been dropped on her by a passing plane, as Fletch had once said. But her smile was warm, tinged though it was with the wry reproach of the Old Friend Neglected.

"I had no idea you were still in New York, because you never answered my letters," Deenie said, picking up her purchase—two rumba dolls. "I always buy my take-home presents here when I get back," she explained. "They're so much nicer than what you see on the cruise. I like to send things to the old crowd. Did you get the basket I sent from Nassau that time I was down there? I thought your husband might like it for his empty bottles."

"You mean Fletch," Liza said, with a sudden memory of a frightful row over that very basket. Fletch had pitched the basket out the window, bringing on the old can't-you-be-at-least-civil-to-my-friends routine. "I've just married again, Deenie. Walker Malin. He's a lawyer."

"How wonderful!" Deenie dropped her package to seize Liza's hands. "I just knew you would change. I felt it in my bones. Come on in here for a cup of tea and tell me all about it. I'm simply dying to hear."

There was no refusing Deenie, who propelled Liza with joyous cries into a rather magnificent bar next door. They sat down at a little table, and Deenie beamed at her. Liza had almost forgotten about Deenie, worn out by the necessity of defending her to her ex-husband, fletch. But now she recalled that one of Fletch's grievances was Deenie's habit of asking for a cup of tea at bars.

"She doesn't drink, so why shouldn't she have tea?" Liza had wearily argued.

"Then why doesn't she go to a tearoom by herself and get it? Why does she have to tag us and embarrass us before bartenders?" Fletch had shouted. This led neatly into "You and your precious bartenders," and then they were off.

Now, the waiter's scowl at Deenie's request for a cup of tea obliged Liza to appease him by ordering a double Martini, just as Fletch used to do. And as Fletch could have predicted, Deenie said the tea wasn't hot enough and must go back.

No wonder waiters hated teetotalers, Liza reflected. Their abstinence seemed miserliness rather than a virtue; their pious preoccupation with their livers was no good reason for bullying waiters and undertipping. Without Fletch on hand to point this out, Liza found herself free to agree with his irritation. That's one for the book, she thought, my agreeing with Fletch about Deenie!

"I always said you should have a really responsible man for a husband," Deenie said enthusiastically. "Naturally, I never said anything at the time you were with Fletcher, but lots of times I wouldn't have blamed you for leaving him, especially when he was being funny—or when he thought he was."

"Oh, he *was* funny, Deenie!" Liza protested. "Fletch could always get me laughing in the middle of an argument—that is, up to the last year or so. Everyone admits he's a real clown."

"I like more of a dry wit," Deenie said, pursing her lips as if she were a wit-taster and could detect the degree of moisture in any clever phrase, domestic or imported. "I'll never forget the time he snipped off the telephone wire right when you were talking to me over the phone. I never considered that a joke, but maybe you did."

It wasn't a joke, Liza recollected with a faint sigh. Fletch was always infuriated when Deenie telephoned just as they were setting out for the theater or a party, delaying them with endless, unimportant chatter. "Deenie's lonely and never has any beaux, and can't I be decent to my oldest friend in New York?" had been Liza's stock retort. That inevitably led to a row that would end with one or the other of them banging out the door.

"I hope your new husband is more settled about money matters," Deenie said, stirring her cup of tea vigorously. ("Now why should she always make all that whoop-de-doo about stirring her tea when she doesn't take sugar?" Fletch used to demand.) It was an irritating mannerism, Liza conceded.

"Those little lines are gone from your face, so I gather that your worries are all over now," Deenie added generously.

True, Liza thought. She certainly didn't have to worry about whether Walker would show up late—broke, in dirty, unpressed clothes, with dreadful newfound chums, ready to offend the most vulnerable and insult the most important—the way Fletch used to do. Walker was a gentleman, to be trusted in those superficial matters that turn out to be basic.

"But what could I do when these people insisted—" Fletch used to explain, in deepest contrition. "I couldn't hurt their feelings."

"So you had to hurt mine!" Liza could hurl back bitterly.

"Would you please bring me another pitcher of hot water?" Liza heard Deenie asking the waiter. "No, not another order of tea. I'll just use the tea bag I have right here."

"Another double Martini," Liza said hastily, smitten by the waiter's fiery glance. "And some caviar, please."

It struck her as funny that she should be reacting to Deenie's restaurant behavior just exactly as Fletch had, though in the past she had coldly rejected his explanation. "Of course," she used to mock him, "you wouldn't dream of drinking all those cocktails if it weren't to offset Deenie's ordering water for her vitamin pills!"

Well, now she saw the point.

"Caviar?" exclaimed Deenie, lifting her eyebrows. "If that's the way it is, then perhaps I can ask if you've forgotten a little deal of ours way back. I really didn't want to bring it up but—"

Liza's pretty mouth opened in consternation.

"Oh *Deenie!* I forgot all about that twenty dollars! That day the c.o.d. came from Altman's and you had to pay it. Fletch didn't have the money at the time. How perfectly awful! I can't imagine myself forgetting such a thing, Deenie. Here—"

Liza opened her purse and was relieved to find she actually could make up the twenty dollars with enough left over for the bar check. She pushed it toward Deenie, who folded it complacently.

"I knew Fletch would forget that money, or claim to forget it, but it wasn't at all like you, Liza," she said. "I wouldn't mention it, but naturally when you ordered caviar—"

"It left my mind completely until this very instant. I can't understand it," Liza said, her face brightly flushed. "I'll never forgive myself for letting you wait all these years. Almost four, isn't it? Oh, I'm so awfully ashamed."

"Maybe Fletch's bad habits were contagious," Deenie laughed. "A good thing that your new husband, Walker, is a good manager."

Liza nodded with pride.

"He is," she said, "and it's such a relief. With Fletch, I never knew where we were, one day to the next. I'd save two dollars on my marketing, and Fletch would give it to a street singer to do 'Mother Machree'—the only thing the man could sing, anyway."

"I remember the very episode," Deenie chuckled. "I would have shot him gladly. Poor Liza. And you had trudged all over Ninth Avenue, feeling so noble over your butcher bargains. I wanted to leave when you started fighting, but I always thought if I didn't stay you'd start whamming each other. I used to stay for your protection."

"I didn't realize Fletch and I seemed so quarrelsome then," Liza observed, surprised. The fact was that they had originally started quarreling only when Deenie came over. Later they got to quarreling at the mere mention of her name; and instead of making up the minute Deenie left, they carried on with increasing bitterness.

Funny, come to think of it, that after all her furious defending of Deenie, the minute Liza got her divorce she never looked up Deenie again. It was Fletch's being so sarcastic about girls' boarding-school friendships that angered her. In reality, she felt just as dashed as Fletch himself when Deenie would drop in uninvited to make a fifth at a carefully arranged little dinner or bridge game. But then Fletch would be so unreasonable about it that someone just had to take the other side.

"I know you were crazy over Fletch," Deenie confessed. "And of course he did have that grin and that Irish charm, but if he'd been mine, that would all have been canceled out by his always being late. The hours you spent waiting for him! His excuses made it even worse."

"I know," Liza was obliged to agree, guiltily recalling that one favorite excuse of Fletch's always had been, "Why hurry, when a little delay might clear Deenie out of the picture."

"I think I fell for Walker because I found I could count on him to the minute," Liza said. "It takes such a load off your mind. Fletch was the kind of man who makes a perfect shrew out of a wife. I was getting to be such a nag that I couldn't even stand myself."

Deenie nodded understandingly, then beckoned the waiter.

"I'd like lemon for my tea, please. And don't you have some potato chips or crackers? No, no, I don't want the menu, I just want those little snacks they have in bars. No point in spoiling my dinner with some expensive order."

"She just sits there with her tea and gobbles up the free lunch," Liza could hear Fletch groan, back in the past. "All I can do is to double up on my own drinks."

"Another Martini, waiter," Liza said feebly, gulping down the last of her cocktail with a vague suspicion she couldn't swallow one more drop.

"How come you've stepped up on your drinking?" Deenie inquired, with a disapproving glance.

Because of you, was on the tip of Liza's tongue, and she thought how Fletch would gloat if he knew he'd finally driven home his point that it was Deenie who made people drink.

Liza was so busy concentrating on her duty to her Martini that she scarcely heard the news Deenie was imparting. Many things had happened to the rest of the girls from Old Gables, it seemed. And none of those things were good. Flo and Sue had been put away, Mabel had ulcers. Their names seemed only dimly familiar to Liza.

"Justine, Georgine, Clarice, Irene, Maxine, Bernice," Liza muttered meditatively. "I know. It's a song. 'At Maxim's Where I Dine.'"

"Why, Liza," Deenie exclaimed reproachfully. "Don't tell me you've forgotten all our old pals at Old Gables. Why, Liza-Liza!"

"Good heavens, Deenie, there are lots of things in my life more important to me than old boarding-school fudge parties," Liza retorted, in exasperation.

Liza almost wished Fletch could see the shocked expression with which Deenie received the remark. Apparently Deenie actually felt that an old school chum had priority over parent, mate, or child, just as Fletch had always complained she did.

"Tell me about Walker," urged Deenie, obviously unaware of the faux pas she had just committed.

"Walker's a Rock of Gibraltar," Liza boasted. "When he says seven-thirty at the Swiss Pavilion, he means seven-thirty and not a minute later. When—" Her eye was held suddenly by the clock over the door, which was frowning away the minutes. "Good heavens, it can't be eight-fifteen! Waiter, check, please! I must run. Oh, dear, Walker will be so worried. Good-bye, Deenie—"

Gloves, purse, check, everything, spilled on the floor in Liza's desperation. She paid no heed to Deenie's queries as to her address and phone number. She tossed her last five-dollar bill on the table and hurried out.

"There are so many things you haven't told me, Liza," Deenie panted behind her. Liza was engaged in trying to flag a cab at the curb, even though the restaurant where Walker was waiting was a bare three blocks away.

Deenie took a large breath of air and asked one last urgent question. "Frankly, how did you finally manage to break with Fletch? Who was the other woman?"

You! Liza wanted to say, but refrained. One of her nylons ripped as she stepped into the cab and her hat fell in the gutter and rolled until Deenie caught it. Liza was ready to cry when the driver snarled at the short trip she indicated.

Deenie threw her a kiss from the curb, but Liza could summon only the palest smile in farewell. She hadn't really liked Deenie a bit, she thought, not since school days. Even back in those days, she thought petulantly, Deenie was always horning into her life just as Fletch had insisted.

At the Swiss Pavilion, she could see Walker sitting at a large corner table and she sent the doorman in to call him out. He emerged, good-looking and self-possessed in spite of the faint surprise in his eyes. He paid the taxi while she babbled explanation.

"But I can't understand how you could come out without a cent, darling," he said gently.

"I didn't. I had thirty dollars, but then I ran into this old school friend, Deenie Bronk, and we stopped for a drink. And I owed her some money—"

"I've been waiting nearly an hour, darling," he said. He was always so calm! Liza thought.

"We agreed on seven-thirty, I thought," he continued. "I was worried."

"But, I tell you, I couldn't get out of it," Liza protested, her voice rising. "After all, Deenie Bronk was my very dearest friend ten years ago, and the least I could do was to have a little cocktail."

"I've never heard you mention her name," Walker said slowly. He took her arm in a firm, protective, masculine grip. "You must have had more than one, dear. And what on earth happened to that hat you're wearing? Not so loud, please, dearest. Everyone's looking at you."

"Let 'em look," Liza cried angrily. "I don't see why a person can't have a little drink with her oldest and dearest friend. And besides, I had to order doubles—Deenie asked for tea."

"Then I should think you would have ordered tea, too," Walker said.

"Of course I couldn't order tea, too," Liza said in exasperation. "I had to order doubles to make up for it. Can't you understand anything?"

She realized that she sounded just like Fletch at his most exasperating moments. But she couldn't help it. She resented Walker's snort of amusement and pulled away from his arm rebelliously. She felt dizzy and injured.

"What do you say to going back to the hotel and having dinner sent up to our apartment?" Walker suggested, his eyes traveling from the disheveled headgear to the torn stocking. "I don't think we can go anywhere, with you like this, honey."

"Like what, may I ask?" Liza shouted indignantly. "If you are criticizing me just because I happened to run into my oldest and dearest friend—"

The echo of the familiar words alerted her brain to all the dangers of the past—and perhaps the dangers of the future, if she didn't take care.

"You're quite right. We'd better go back to the hotel," she said meekly. "Do forgive me for messing up our evening, dear. I'm so sorry."

After all, what was the sense of letting Deenie wreck this marriage, too? Going home, the teas trickled down her cheek. Walker thought it was the Martinis, but it wasn't. Liza was thinking about her first husband. She was beginning to feel acquainted with him.

The Pilgrim

O N THE AFTERNOON OF the third day out, there was a French movie in that pretty hall on top of the boat, first class that is to say, and Miss Harvey thought she ought to go on account of what the French did for us in the Revolution. The leading man in it was Maurice Chevalier, a Frenchman she'd heard about, but he must have fallen on bad times, because he was in filthy old rags and seemed not even to have any handkerchief. Probably had thrown away all his savings on women and horses, the way Those people always did, never thinking of a rainy day. Everybody else seemed to find it very funny, but then They would, it being a French ship. After fidgeting through half of the film, Miss Harvey tiptoed past a row of nuns and went on deck looking for someone who would chat. Three men were writing letters in the library but they did not look up, and the steward in charge seemed to be asleep at his desk.

Miss Harvey cleared her throat.

"Is it allowed for me to take a book to my cabin?" she asked at random.

The young man opened his eyes which were quite bloodshot.

"Which book do you wish to take, Madame?" he asked.

Miss Harvey was confused.

"None in particular," she said, and as he looked at her in a funny way she added, "I didn't bring my reading glasses on this trip. Doctor Fletcher doesn't want me to do any reading."

The young man muttered something, closed his eyes and dropped his head in his hands again. Miss Harvey, a little discomfited, was relieved to see the California girl from her table just outside. She, too, was with Father Moriarity's group of pilgrims to Rome, but she was going straight to Italy instead of stopping off for England and Ireland as the rest of the group was doing. Miss Harvey wished she had thought of doing this; she had visited Ireland once as a girl, and it was a dirty place, although nowadays even the British went there, for some reason.

"It's the only place the children can get enough to eat," that young Englishwoman in the green jersey suit had explained last night, and Miss Harvey's stomach had leaped with apprehension at this threat of no double portions for four whole days in London. She was a good mother, that young Englishwoman, staying in the ship nursery with her children all afternoon to see that they had first turns at the horses and bicycles. All out for England, too, of course, advising Miss Harvey to buy her woolens at some London store, but then They were all out for the Dollar.

"Don't let them rook you," nice Mr. Carey at the bank had warned her. "Save your money for Italy where everything is cheaper. In England they're after our dollars and everything costs almost as much as it does right here. Remember, don't give more than two dollars to each of the stewards."

"I just want to give them enough so that they won't *look* at me," Miss Harvey had wistfully confided. "I just hate the way they *look* at me whatever I give them in foreign countries."

The California girl was in a hurry and said she had just met the Monseigneur in first class who was conducting the 4:15 Mass now if Miss Harvey wanted to go. She was on her way down to her cabin for something to put on her head. Miss Harvey had had the good sense to keep her hat on from morning till night because that way she could always dart into Mass when there was nobody to talk to.

"Do you realize there are four different orders of nuns on board?" the California girl cried out happily, pausing for a moment at top of the stairs. "Two different branches of the Assumption, one Sacred Heart, and all the rest Saint Joseph. Isn't it wonderful?"

A group of priests were studying some map on the wall and Miss Harvey went up to them.

"What time will we pass Newfoundland?" she asked. They turned to her smiling, uncomprehending, and then she remembered someone saying that these were all French Canadians mostly from Quebec. The tall young Austrian she had accosted on deck this morning was just passing and translated her question. It fussed Miss Harvey because she suddenly remembered he was the one who had told her they had already passed Newfoundland. He had been very polite for a German, and when the deck steward had told her she was using the gentleman's deck chair, the German had said Madame was welcome to use it at any time since she had none of her own. He had been very interesting, too, though of course we should have smashed them all to smithereens years ago and would have, too, if it hadn't been for the Roosevelts, and he had said if she went to Germany she should go to the southern part because it was full of flowers and so beautiful that even the peasants went around ringing little bells.

One of the priests was pointing out something on the map but Miss Harvey told the German to explain that she didn't have her glasses. They had strange faces, these French Canadian priests, sort of strong and wild and dark, not rosy and delicate like those she knew in Boston, and when they laughed they sounded like harsh sea birds. To tell the truth they were a disappointing lot, forty of them, too, all pilgrims, and not a one who spoke English, but then They were not very bright up there. In the little chapel they held masses from crack of dawn till bedtime to give each one of them a chance, but it was no fun attending Mass when you couldn't have a friendly chat with the priest later. Very queer they didn't speak English when Canada was an English possession (though it would have been ours if it hadn't been for the Roosevelts).

Miss Harvey approached her cabin without enthusiasm. Her cabin mate, Miss Forest, would probably be in there lying down or washing her hair or studying her French. You couldn't talk to her because she always had some snippy answer. Miss Harvey had viewed her companion with apprehension the first day, for the girl was in her twenties and likely to be banging in and out all night with boys, drinking and smoking and playing the ukulele. She wasn't pretty, of course, not in the least, not as Miss Harvey herself had been at that long ago age. This girl was a good five feet eleven with stout muscular legs, short sandy hair, a kind of boyish round face, big white teeth, and black-rimmed spectacles. She was a research worker, whatever that was, from Michigan she had said, and she was going to do some more research at the Sorbonne. She seemed uneasy about her wardrobe on the trip, always changing her sweaters and scarves as if that would make her look any better, tying a red ribbon around her hair then taking it off, changing her glasses to green-rimmed ones for dinner, then, as she had done last night, deciding she didn't feel well enough for dinner, anyway. At the very first Miss Harvey had thought they might get on since Miss Forest had gone to Radcliffe for two years and Miss Harvey felt that living in the same town sort of gave her a Radcliffe degree herself, just as she felt it made her a Harvard man, a Lowell, a Cabot. But Miss Forest hadn't appreciated Boston, had even said that she considered it the Deep South culturally, a remark Miss Harvey knew meant something or other unpleasant.

Sure enough there was Miss Forest—she had said to call her Nancy but Miss Harvey ignored this overture, knowing it meant she would be called by *her* first name in no time—with a towel around her hair, indicating she had washed it again.

"It usually has a natural wave when I wash it," she explained apologetically, "only it didn't work out yesterday so I did it again."

"Horse-racing in the lounge at four-thirty," said Miss Harvey brightly. "I won four dollars on the Trinidad cruise."

"You can't get near it on account of your priests," answered Miss Forest, rubbing her scalp carefully with a circular motion.

"Don't call them *my* priests, not those French Canadians," said Miss Harvey. "Anyway they have little enough pleasure, poor dears."

"They all look so happy," reflected Miss Forest. "They go around with broad smiles on their faces, like old people do in Miami. I guess this pilgrimage is the first time they've ever had a trip. I only hope they last till they get to Rome."

Miss Harvey always made a point of never arguing with cabin mates. If they were noisy or dirty you simply went to the captain and changed cabins, and when they were satisfactory in ordinary respects but contrary-minded as this girl was, you just kept out of their way and never answered.

"Why should the priests have all the worldly pleasures, and those nice-looking nuns have to stay in their cabins? I'm a feminist," said Miss Forest, answering herself since Miss Harvey merely went on changing her good black jersey to the purple woolen she wore for dress with her mother's sapphires. "Of course, women never go into anything unless they believe in it completely and are prepared to follow the line. Men figure they are always justified in wangling whatever they want.... You have a very pretty figure."

"Thank you, I take plenty of exercise," Miss Harvey said, standing in her slip before the mirror, knowing perfectly well her legs and body, at sixty-five, were perfectly proportioned, though the only men who knew this were her physicians. Sometimes, when she heard her brothers and their friends exclaim over some bathing beauty she smiled to herself, satisfied that she looked better than any of the ladies they admired. It used to give her a perverse pleasure to refuse to go swimming in public or wear slacks. On the other hand she was not prudish with women when close quarters made modesty ridiculous, but stripped as casually as anyone else, particularly before a strapping, lumpy girl like Nancy Forest.

"The woman across the hall is Russian," said Nancy. She wished she could help from seeming so—so *loutish,* really; maybe it had to do with always having to wear oversizes; even your remarks never fitted into any conversation without bursting something or other.

"I've talked to her," said Miss Harvey agreeably. "She knows Newton Center well, summers on the Cape, and she hates the present Russian government. Maybe she's a spy the way They always are. She said I would have loved Russia under the Czar. Things were very different, everyone spoke French and people were not killed for little trivial things, they were only sent to Siberia. She was sitting with that French woman in the sort of bear fur coat, that one who seems very educated, speaks French beautifully, very fast, the way that educated sort always does."

"She's the mother of those two loud girls in velvet slacks always yelling and running around," said Nancy. "The ones we thought were Americans."

"They've been touring the Rockies this summer and they're traveling in the coach," said Miss Harvey, who knew everything; it was really frightening, Nancy thought. "Their names are Renée and Adrienne but now they call themselves Micky and Johnny, their mother says and they said it was more fun going third class, but she's very strict, not like American mothers, still it was cheaper so she let them do it. In a way the Russians are better than the French. The French always use their hands so, of course they're very thrifty. I just went down and looked in the coach but it looks very dingy."

"Tourist, not coach," said Nancy, as if it made any difference, there was no use pinning down any of Miss Harvey's thoughts. She shook out her hair but again the wave hadn't come back in and it hung limply; still it had a nice sheen. When it fell down over her eyes in the laboratory sometimes as she worked, Professor Marriot used to laugh and say, "Nancy, you look absolutely beautiful when you concentrate like that." She always had some answer, such as, "Yes, a girl always looks beautiful when she's working overtime so the boss can go to a party." She wished she could stop saying things like that, especially since a look of having been slapped sometimes came over Marriot's face. Maybe in France not knowing the language well would be a godsend.

"I wish I was going to England like you," she said suddenly.

Miss Harvey adjusted the sapphire clip at her throat in exactly the spot her mother and grandmother had always worn it, and put on her sapphire velvet toque. Out of the corner of her eye she could see Miss Forest looking at her, combing away with a look of naked desolation. She felt she was doing the girl a favor by having a wrinkled neck and face and using no makeup on them, either, to simulate youth. As a matter of fact, she used to see no harm in makeup, but she observed in her travels that strange men are a little leary of older women wearing lipstick, whereas her gray hair and decent oldness gave her respectful attention from whomsoever she cared to approach. An old lady could go anywhere, do anything, *speak* to anyone, providing she never went into bars or used make-up or strong perfume. Like a priest, really. Sometimes Miss Harvey felt sorry for lonely men her age who dared not strike up conversations with the other sex, particularly the younger ones they liked, without being suspect.

"A young woman isn't safe traveling alone in England," Miss Harvey said. "They always tell you about the French and Italians molesting girls alone on the street, but all they do is pinch you a little bit, but your Englishman sees a girl alone and he doesn't bother to pinch, he marches right up and makes a proposition in plain language."

"I wonder what would happen if the girl pinched back," reflected Miss Forest, putting on her green-rimmed glasses with as much care as her companion had adjusted her sapphires.

"The French and Italians are more polite to your face, generally," pursued Miss Harvey, waiting patiently for Miss Forest, who seemed to think she'd made some joke, to stop laughing. "But, I suppose they don't have those lasting feelings the way the English have—they're all very superficial."

She disliked the way Miss Forest shut her mouth, sort of smiling, as if she could say something but wouldn't. It puzzled her that the girl never talked to anyone, for she certainly seemed opinionated enough. True, she herself, as a girl, indeed up to about ten years ago, had been afraid to mix with strangers, but that was because men were always making advances. Miss Forest hardly needed to worry on that score. She was big enough to scare them off. Not that she looked any plainer than the other young people aboard, for they were an ugly, unkempt lot the way young people now always were.

"Why don't you go upstairs and mix with some other young folks?" Miss Harvey suggested, adding artlessly, "It looks to me as if there were a lot of research workers among them."

Nancy laughed mirthlessly.

"I think I know what you mean," she said, and then with an effort to be friendly said, "I think you're wonderful the way you can just go and talk to anybody, and travel all over having a good time all by yourself."

"Being in the Church does give you an advantage," Miss Harvey explained primly. "You can always talk to the fathers or the sisters or ask people about services. Of course this year being Holy Year makes everybody traveling much more friendly, too, you can talk to people just back from Rome or other pilgrims with your group."

"Don't try to convert me," Nancy exclaimed brusquely. "Besides there are other kinds of pilgrims aboard. Did you see those boys in Tourist on their way to Israel?"

She was being unnecessarily nasty, Nancy reminded herself, knowing that Miss Harvey regarded the others as sort of common-law pilgrims, not to be censured, but to be decently ignored.

"In our faith we never try to convert," Miss Harvey said quietly. She considered whether she should go up for the Monseigneur's Mass, but the truth was she didn't like his looks. He was probably a very fine man but he looked like nothing at all, square and toadish like Bishop O'Malley, and like him with no dignity at all, always wasting time on just anybody, probably thinking that was being Christian. Now you take a man like Bishop Vincent, God rest his soul, who looked just like John Barrymore (before the latter took to drink, that is) and never lowered himself to mix with the rabble, always keeping his dignity so that it was an honor to know him, there was somebody to admire. None of the young priests could come up to him.

"You ought to stay up tonight and watch the dancing," said Miss Harvey pleasantly, and started out. "I see that nice German just came down so I can take his chair."

Now what will she find out, Nancy meditated irritably. She goes swooping about this ship like a hungry gull, I see her all over the place, darting into a clutch of priests, hovering over some party and then down into the midst, and it's peck, peck, peck and up she comes with some little fish or bit of garbage, scraps of everything and everybody under the sun, all mixed up. Watch the dancing, indeed, deliberately sticking your neck out to be a wallflower when the one thing you could do was dance—that is if anyone ever asked you, which was hardly likely when you were usually a head taller than any man except Marriot.

I wish I was little and old and gray! she thought passionately, and then was ashamed of being jealous of poor little Miss Harvey who could talk to anybody, who didn't worry what people might think of her because she knew she was better than anybody else, she had Family, Boston, Age, and the Church. It was perfectly ridiculous, Nancy thought, and there was no reason a girl of her brains and sense shouldn't make the most of them. Twenty-nine, her first trip to Paris—and jealous of a poor old spinster. Nancy jammed the green-rimmed glasses in her pocket, tied the scarf Marriot's wife had given her around her neck, and marched resolutely up on deck. She saw the two tall sisters of St. Joseph striding up and down and was suddenly warmed when one of them smiled at her. They were both taller than she was, strong strapping women, maybe from Newfoundland fisherman families. In civilian life they would have been gawky, self-conscious girls, too big for beaux, probably desperately poor besides, with no future but hard work and self-sacrifice. But the convent robes made them proud and unafraid, no one could laugh at their clumsiness, they lived an enchanted life, respected, admired. Nancy rehearsed mentally the French sentence that was to thank the one who had given her the Dramamine pills for seasickness the first day. Breathlessly she stopped them on their next turn and tried out her French on the smiling nun, then retreated, quite overcome by her success. The pretty young French girls in slacks and lumber jackets raced past her with Miss Harvey's German and the blond Frenchman in the blond corduroys. She would try talking to them, too, Nancy vowed, but they were in a huddle laughing together. *Scoot,* they kept saying, *scoot, voilà la scoot.* One of them seemed to be smiling at her, but just as she was about to smile back Nancy thought with consternation, They mean *me,* they're saying I'm a girl scout! She looked down at the ocean swirling below, the waves crackling into the same radiant blue of the nun's ribbon; she could feel it sucking her down into the blue and now she wished it would, especially since she felt she was going to be sick again. *Scoot,* she said to herself, and stumbled down to the cabin again just as Miss Harvey was connecting up with the two exchange students going from U. of L.A. to Cambridge.

The good thing about Dramamine was that it knocked you out. You sank deeper and deeper into oceans of sleep, you knew you were missing dinner, and once in a while a crash of glasses and your head bumping on the side table indicated a storm was coming up and it was wonderful having that excuse for staying in bed maybe forever. Lights went on and the steward came in and there was Miss Harvey, getting ready for bed so it must be late, fixing the luggage and jars so they wouldn't crash. Finally Nancy opened her eyes and squinted at her wristwatch. Midnight. The steward left and Miss Harvey locked the door. Nancy watched her cautiously climbing into her berth, wearing the lacy mauve chiffon nightie—definitely French, definitely expensive, Nancy thought, clutching her own blue flannel pajama coat around her throat.

"It was so rough they had to stop dancing," Miss Harvey stated. "I felt a little queer myself—not sick, because I never give in to being sick—just sort of queer."

Good for you, Nancy thought bitterly. Miss Harvey lay back on her pillow, the light showing her clear-cut patrician face faintly green.

"It's really dangerous, you know, this storm. Mr. Carey said never to worry, though, just give the steward two dollars and he'll look after you in case of anything," she said, and then mused dreamily, "I suppose the Captain is up there on the bridge right in the thick of it. Oh, I'd give anything to be up there!"

"No!" burst out of Nancy in spontaneous alarm. "You can't go up *there,* Miss Harvey! I mean—it's not that dangerous."

"Of course not," answered Miss Harvey cheerfully. "No need to worry, because our Annapolis men are probably all up there taking charge."

"Not on the French line, Miss Harvey," Nancy groaned.

"Perhaps not," conceded Miss Harvey politely, but not at all convinced. "Do you know those two men at the next table who looked so nice are just newspaper men? I chatted with them and they're really very nice, didn't smoke or spit the way they usually do."

It was too bad Miss Harvey wasn't a Protestant, Nancy reflected, it would give her such a marvelous opportunity for "Theying" in Rome. They, they, they, they, she thought drowsily sinking into sleep again, they, they, they, but who is *we?* Who could possibly be *we* so far as Miss Harvey was concerned? But what am I thinking about, Nancy reminded herself, when I've never been *we* either, no matter how I tried.

Wonderful Dramamine, she thought next morning, too late for breakfast, Miss Harvey long ago up and out, pecking over the passengers, in and out of the chapel, praying, pecking, praying, pecking. Taking out her walking shoes from the closet, Nancy thought they looked like some lumberjack's compared to the tiny gray suedes of Miss Harvey's. It was late enough to go to the dining room for lunch, too early for Miss Harvey, but the two newspapermen were already there at the next table, arguing intently with each other as they always were. How had Miss Harvey been able to break in on them, but then it was always the same method: *You're going to Rome of course? What, no? I understood you were with our pilgrimage. May I join you? I had the address of a shop in Florence where you get darling leather things awfully cheap and I lost it. I wonder if you could tell me*—They were young men, just Nancy's age, and she could hear them talking about the *Star* and she wished she dared ask them if they knew Mary or Steve, and what they thought of Marriot's weekly letter. Then Miss Harvey came in and she couldn't hear what they were talking about anymore.

"You know that colored man always writing in the library—" Miss Harvey was chattering away. "I thought of course he was a Hindu or Filipino but when I said something to him it turns out he's only from New York, you wouldn't think on a high-class boat like this—but then They always—"

They, they. It was really too much. Nancy finished her coffee and went up on deck. The young French girls and the exchange students were taking pictures of each other and they were all laughing and joking in French. No matter how hard she studied the language she would be left out, Nancy thought, and she'd let herself in for a whole year of it. One of the priests came hurrying out, excitedly collecting a group of his brothers to go in and see the Clark Gable picture in the cinema. Nancy caught a glimpse of her cabin mate darting resolutely after them, saw one of them pause and answer her as she scampered alongside. A girl with tousled yellow curls and a huge beaver jacket approached, and Nancy braced herself to be friendly but she only wanted her to move aside in order to take a snapshot of the two journalists behind her. *Scoot,* Nancy was sure she heard the word again, *scoot!* She stared at the sea fixedly. After a while she caught sight of Miss Harvey flying out from the cinema.

"Wasn't the picture any good?" Nancy asked.

"Just terrible! It was auto racing and it's so dangerous," gasped Miss Harvey. "I just hate it but of course Clark Gable, being a regular he-man like he is, probably likes that sort of thing, but one of these days he'll get killed and then where will his family be? Of course, I understand he has taken out annuities, so he won't have to go around in rags like that French actor yesterday, but auto racing is too *dangerous!*"

Her eyes were sweeping the deck, looking for more promising conversation. She spotted the Monseigneur and was gone in a flash.

"Are we past Newfoundland yet?" Nancy heard her beseech him.

Scoot, the mocking words reached her again from the laughing young people behind her, and indeed they were looking at her, no mistake about it. It was her brown tweeds and her tallness and her woolen stockings and the big brown pigskin bag over her shoulder, and they didn't mean any harm. Nancy stared down at the ocean, leaning over the deck rail, wishing for the refuge of seasickness again. All next year would be like this voyage, she told herself, with no dear ocean to give her an excuse for retreat. The two tall sisters of St. Joseph paused beside her in their march, and Nancy realized with sudden elation that they wanted to talk to her.

"I speak the English, Mademoiselle," the smiling one volunteered. "I hope you are over the seasickness. Sister Elizabeth remark that Mademoiselle is even as big as we are, and maybe it will not be easy to find the big shoes for walking in Rome, so we just give you an address for your convenience. You are with our pilgrimage, yes?"

Now she was walking between them down the deck, the three tall women against the world, and Nancy felt herself dreamily sinking under oceans of Dramamine, safe from everything.

"I—I—" she heard her voice ever so faintly—"Yes, I would like to be."

PART III

Every Day Is Ladies' Day

$\mathcal{A}$T FIRST HE THOUGHT he wouldn't go at all. Stand her up. Let the dinner get cold waiting for him. Let her find out she could not ignore an old friend for years and then call him up just because she needed an extra man for dinner. On second thought, the longer dinner waited the more cocktails they'd have, the better-natured they'd be, and there was the chance that by the time they sat down to dinner no one would even notice his absence!

He liked Clara after all, liked her a lot. He had known her for years—knew her in Paris after the First World War—knew her husbands—liked them all—still had some fine suits Number Three had given him—had the tailor nip them in at the waist a little and they fitted perfectly.

"What's happened to you and Clara?" people used to ask when it got around he was no longer invited to Clara's parties.

"I just couldn't take it anymore," he would answer. "After all, I've known Clara a long time and I just couldn't take it."

The truth was he was terribly pleased at the thought of seeing her again, in spite of everything. He never understood what he had done to make her chill toward him, but figured that it was the war that had come between them. Her house was always filled with soldiers and sailors, and she had been having too good a time to think of him. Now that they had all gone back to their wives and girls there were extra places at good tables once again. He was tired of being asked to artists' homes on the strength of his museum connection, tired of listening to wives try to sell him their husbands' work, the artists themselves displaying integrity by elaborate insults. He had about as much power to buy as the checkroom attendants and told them so, but they never let go. At least Clara wasn't interested in art; he had to give her credit for that. He had a lot of funny stories to tell her about their old Paris chums. All of them in loony bins or sanitariums, the ones that weren't on Nembutal.

"I used to look for my friends in the society columns," he intended to say tonight. "Now I look for them on the barbituary page."

Go? Of course he'd go. He took a last look in the mirror, brushes in hand. Chip Thomas, who was picking him up at Clara's request, stood in the doorway, waiting.

"What's this, Tully? Do I see a gray hair there?" Chip inquired.

"If you do I get my money back," Tully said grimly, and slipped a carnation in his lapel.

They went downstairs and met the doorman bringing the pooch back. She was five years old but still flung herself at Tully like a pup whenever she saw him. Dogs never learned.

"Listen, honey," Tully said to her. "Tonight I'll bring you back something good. How about some 'long pig'? But don't sit up for me, honey. It may take a little time to wear out my welcome."

The dog was still laughing heartily as the elevator went up.

Chip looked around the lobby, a pleasant little lounge, and then glanced curiously at Tully.

"This is a nice little joint. Better than where I last saw you," he commented. "I guess you're getting ahead. But how?"

"The way any young man gets ahead," Tully said. "White tie and driver's license."

He did not know Chip Thomas very well, beyond seeing him at a few parties, nor did he know how well Chip knew Clara. Better not to trust anybody much until you knew them; then, not at all. Chip was much younger than he, around thirty-five maybe, but he was stout whereas Tully had kept his figure and his smooth complexion, and as he often said, most of his favorite hairs. He could pass for thirty-five unless someone that age was around.

As soon as Chip pulled his car up at Clara's charming little house Tully felt a surge of joy such as he had not known in years. He whistled a gay tune.

"Imagine you remembering 'The Red Mill'!" Chip observed drily.

"Only the revival," Tully answered, not at all offended; and then confided, "The old war horse smells the powder. Prewar liquor, roast beef, cognac, beautiful girls, cigars, cigarettes, candy, chewing gum."

"She's lucky she still has the place," Chip said.

"Women never lose anything," Tully said. "You know that, old boy."

It was one of the many Smallest Houses in New York—two tiny rooms on each of the four floors and a dining room off a basement garden where a pink plaster birdbath, large enough to accommodate one humming bird or two well-adjusted bumblebees, nestled in a circle of green potted plants.

"Herbs," Tully nodded to Chip, happy that nothing had changed. "She always keeps a pot of basil around for some pinheaded lover. Clara still likes Keats, poor darling."

They left their hats with the tiny maid in the dining room and went upstairs to the diminutive drawing room. Walls and windows were muffled in pink-and-cream-colored hangings just as they used to be.

"Clara loves candy," Tully whispered to Chip. "Nobody but Clara could live forever in a grocery treat. The dwarf's room is to your left, old man."

"I know," Chip said huffily. "I've been here before."

A quick casing of the room showed that Clara had reached the cautious state where she invited women her own age. There was only one possible female, a blond still charmingly awkward and bony, her mother probably praising Allah for the long-hair fashion that softened so many hard young faces. Not bad. He knew nobody, which must mean that Clara was coming up in the world. As she left the fireside group to greet them he saw at once that she had aged; laughter and love had left their mark.

"Darling!" he cried, kissing her loudly in midair. "You look marvelous. What have you *done* to yourself?"

"You know perfectly well I'm in my dotage, you monster," Clara murmured with a muscular handshake, a new affectation, Tully thought. It occurred to him much later that she barely spoke to Chip, and he was rather proud of his unselfishness in bringing it to her attention.

"Be nice to Chip, darling," he whispered as they went down to dinner. "He's stuffy and I know what you mean, but honey, you're getting on and men don't grow on bushes."

"I happen to have a green thumb, dear," Clara said. "But thanks just the same."

He thought that if he was going to start in again with Clara's crowd he would certainly mention to her that no matter what marvels the cook had prepared everyone would have sacrificed them for another round of cocktails. Fortunately, he was in such a good humor that he could keep up the conversation during

dinner single-handed without the extra stimulant, but he noticed
Chip and the four other men present were silent and gloomy, not
at all cheered by the carefully selected bad wine. To relieve the
situation and show Clara he was still the best friend she had ever
had, he lifted his goblet in a toast to her, adding jokingly, "I knew
Clara when she had *good* wines."

No use denying that she did have a darn good table. The
sauces were familiar even if the guests were not. He had two help-
ings of everything and slipped an extra piece of the roast into his
napkin to take home to the pooch, though she might not like the
Burgundian sauce. By great good fortune he was seated next to
the McCullen girl, the nice kid, who obviously was taken by him
but scared to death of her mother, a fish-looking dame in poison
green about Clara's age who was stuck with Chip Thomas. It
seemed little Felicia was studying painting and was delightfully
impressed by his being at the museum. She said she was nineteen,
but he thought she was a good twenty-three, if she was a day, and
not helped by her bouffant baby-blue subdeb frock. She was
adorably uncurved and had a way of looking up at him sidewise
whenever he spoke that actually thrilled him. Her mother kept a
sharp eye on him, and the minute he had a chance he murmured
to Clara it wasn't fair to the kid to invite the mother along to parties. But Clara was dense about a lot of little things and didn't always take suggestions in the right spirit. You couldn't lose four
husbands without getting irritable.

"I understand Mr. Tully is at the museum, Felicia," the
mother said. She would! "Why not ask him to help you get an
exhibition?"

"I've known Tully for twenty-five years," Clara said, "and I've
never known him to do anything for anybody."

"Now, Clara, old dear," he reproached her playfully, "if I'd
known you were going to be yourself, I never would have
come. You know Clara's husband, the one that lasted four

years—Harvey, wasn't it?—used to say he could stand all of Clara's moods except the times when she was being herself. I always liked Harvey. He was my favorite."

"One person's meat is another person's poison," Clara murmured a bit sulkily.

"If I remember rightly you divorced Harvey when you discovered that one person's meat was *everybody's* meat," he chuckled, with a wink at Chip.

"You should know," Clara retorted, never able to take kidding. "You were the one who told me all about it."

He was feeling too good to pick her up on that, so all he said was, "Oh, but I didn't tell you even *half* about it, old dear."

"Old dear yourself," Clara snapped.

It struck him right away that both Clara and the girl's mother were miffed at him for devoting himself to the youngster. The mother, you could see, fancied herself for having kept her complexion and figure (such as they were) and naturally resented having a young rival always around. He'd seen it happen a dozen times and knew from experience that the diplomatic thing was to butter up the old girl for a while, just to keep her from taking it out on the kid.

"Next time you go shopping for your daughter, why not invite me to come along, Mrs. McCullen?" he suggested courteously. "Have you ever tried dressing her in black?"

The old girl gave him a sweet smile. "Felicia dresses herself now, Mr. Tully," she answered. "Felicia, dear, would you like Mr. Tully to take you shopping to pick out a black snowsuit?"

"For black snowstorms," he added quickly, turning what might have been a nasty crack into a good-natured laugh.

But the old lady had scared the kid so that she carefully applied herself to the old codger on her other side all during dessert. It suited Tully since it gave him a chance to go to town on the really superb mousse. He was sorry he'd teased Clara, come to think of it. He shouldn't have risked her dropping him again. It seemed the old codger had something to do with the San Francisco Museum and might, on Clara's say-so, get him a position there. He mentioned this to her on the way up to the drawing room for coffee, cleverly suggesting that he drop in next Sunday for tea, say, and talk it over, perhaps have the little McCullen kid, too. But please, he added, no Chip Thomas. A good fellow, all right, but a complete moron. Hadn't got the point of even one of his stories, not even the dude-ranch one.

"He seemed to get it the first time you told it," Clara said. "It lost a little, I myself felt, in the retelling. Try it again over coffee."

He did not take this up but switched to the subject of Felicia. The kid was attractive, he admitted, but it was pretty tough on her with the old lady so jealous. It was a darned shame, he said, because the old lady could ruin the kid's chances with some men who didn't see through her game. Clara stubbornly refused to see the point, of course.

"The 'old lady,' as you call her, is five years younger than you, darling," she said in her haughtiest British accent.

He hoped that in spite of her pique she would have to admit the party would have been a dismal flop without him. He had to rack his brain to keep the talk going, and in one lull he had to catch himself before getting into the dude-ranch story again. Not his fault. It was just that everyone was waiting for Clara to get out the brandy. Sensing this, Tully decided the only way to save the situation was to joke about it, so he said, patting Clara genially on the back, "Crack out the stuff, old dear. We all know you've got it."

Even the brandy could not liven the dreary little group and Tully constantly had to snatch the talk from the somber subjects started by the others, resorting to that old reliable attention-getter—"Clara will kill me for telling this but..."—or—"I swore I would never tell this to a living soul, but since we're all friends..."

He obtrusively filled his glass from time to time for sheer fuel purposes; and once, when Chip Thomas forgot to put it back where it belonged, Tully fell over a footstool snatching it back. Everyone laughed and Tully thought: What a bunch of morons! Here I am knocking myself out to entertain them, but I have to have a concussion before they'll laugh.

He was glad that they started to leave soon after ten, and he had optimistic visions of a cozy threesome—Clara (necessarily), himself, and the adorable girl. Yes, by Jove, he had really fallen for her, and he was pretty sure he had made a good impression from the way she looked at him. If he ever should marry—and he might when his wardrobe wore out—he would take a chance on a fresh unspoiled little creature like this, perhaps Felicia herself.

But before he could wangle this little scheme the mother had whisked Felicia away, leaving only himself and Chip Thomas to sit up with Clara.

"You don't need to stay on my account, old man," Tully said to Chip, translating a significant look in Clara's eyes. "I can always get a cab."

The least he could do for Clara, he thought, was help her get rid of her dull guests, though it meant he had to give up the free ride home in Chip's car. Oh, well...

Clara slipped a hand over Chip's. "Don't worry about him, Chip," she murmured. "As he says, he can get a cab." (She must have been drinking.) "He can find one on Third Avenue and, that means you can stay on for a little after-party talk with Mama, just our twosy-woosies."

It was as blunt as that. Tully could hardly believe his ears, but he was obliged to take the hint, especially since Clara fairly flew out to get his hat. He could have killed Chip Thomas for lolling back on the sofa as if he owned the place.

"Looks to me as if Clara's sore at me about something," Tully said with a wry laugh. "I wish I knew what it was."

"Oh, pay it no mind," Chip said airily. "She's always picked on you, I gather from all you've been saying."

Of course she always had—come to think of it—but why? Tully puzzled over it all the way home, and it was not until he was dividing his roast-beef sandwich with the pooch that the answer came.

What a sap I am! he thought. Why, of course! It's just because I never made a pass at her, that's all!

It was so simple he laughed out loud. Thank God, he could still read women!

The Glads

HE HAD THOUGHT HE knew just what to expect from a family rout like this, but his premonitions had been but the toy model for the monster production. Certainly the Bateses were a huge family with many ramifications, and naturally in his twenty years absence they would have multiplied, but who would have pictured this enormous crowd spilling over the house onto the great lawn, their cars lined up for a whole block, traffic and program instructions rasping out through a public address system? Everything was louder and grander than he, in his naive New York ignorance, could remember or even imagine. He had heard that Stan had done well (probably doing six or seven thousand a year now, he had guessed), and had bought "a nice home in a nice residential district," as his mother had written. He had visualized the conventional suburban house, Westchester style, on a decent side street cuddling as close as possible to the second-best boulevard. Nothing had prepared him for the spacious ranch house, sprawling its dozen rooms and five-car garage over half an acre of landscaped green.

Stan *would* have a ranch house, no matter what it was, Allan thought. He always went for those catchy sales words that made ordinary things sound special and important. Phrases like "plunging neckline," "fan out of Chicago," "snap brim," "dynaflow." Of course it would have to be a "ranch house."

He had never expected to be envious of Stan Rice and the idea depressed him. He found himself wishing he had come back a year ago when his suit was new, or five years ago when he was riding high, or two years ago before he had turned in the Lincoln for his second-hand Chevy, and was still married to Betsy Brown, Hollywood actress. Suddenly everything he had achieved, the self-confidence built on the admiration of colleagues and pride in his expeditions, left him. He had been braced for stupidity and indifference to what his name now stood for, but he'd never dreamed of being reduced in one moment to a childish feeling of helpless inadequacy.

I might have known the place would always get me like this, he thought, disgusted with himself. I knew I should never come back.

He had come back only to see Corinne, but now he wondered if he could ever get to her through the mob. He looked twice at each young girl with shining black hair or bright blue eyes, thinking it must be Corinne's daughter, though these features were common to all the Bates women. The chances were that Corinne's daughter would not have her mother's looks. Corinne had kept hers, so his mother had written. If he had to come back at all he wished he had come back last summer when he could have seen Corinne alone. She was the only one in the whole family he gave a damn for, and if she hadn't been his first cousin he might have married her, but you didn't get away from your family by marrying back into it, at least he had had that much sense.

All the way up the front walk, through the porch groups, and into the house he was halted by vaguely familiar voices crying out, "Allan, where on earth did you come from?" Each time he had to explain that he happened to be driving west anyway, and had decided to stop over on the spur of the moment. Each time it took a little while to figure out which nephew, cousin, or neighbor had spoken. He fancied he could spot Corinne's husband's family, by the sandy hair and Hoosier accents. He recognized Stan himself, heavier, grayer, but not greatly changed, towering over a group in the room beyond, complaining in his high, nasal voice, "The music alone cost me four hundred dollars, but everybody's making such a hullaballoo you can't even hear it."

"The Mayor came just before we got here," a thin colorless young woman exclaimed happily, very dressed up in white hat, navy suit, white kid gloves and handbag. "I'll bet Stan's set up over that. Why Allan Bates! It is Allan, isn't it? Don't you remember me, your little cousin Ruby, second cousin that is? Why everybody's here, it seems like! Look, Aunt Lou, aren't you glad you came now? Just see who's here all the way from Pittsburgh."

"New York," Allan corrected her patiently.

The wizened little old woman beside him whose palsy kept the weird bird on her hat in a state of perpetual animation shook Allan's hand, peering suspiciously up into his face as if wary of impostors.

"We've got plenty of Bateses in New York City," she stated. "Two of them ran for office right there in the state of New York. The Bateses are well-thought-of wherever they are."

"Allan's done very well, too, don't forget," Cousin Ruby reminded her. "Wasn't there something in the paper about you just a little while ago?"

"There was," Allan admitted. "it was about Betsy Brown divorcing me for mental cruelty. That was last October."

"That long ago?" asked Ruby with a vague smile. "Well, I still work in the library at Wooster Center. I took two days off to come here, and it's really worth it. All the Cleveland Bateses came, folks I haven't seen for years. Cousin Tracy came in his own plane. He's in there now with Stan. You remember Cousin Tracy and Ed."

"If you're leaving by way of Corning, maybe you'd drive me back to the Home," Aunt Lou suggested to Allan. "It would save me taxi."

"Good grief, I wish you wouldn't always have to bring up the fact that you live in a Home, Aunt Lou!" Ruby said irritably. "You'll make Allan think the family back here is going to seed."

"No, I wouldn't think that," Allan said.

"I'll have you know it's quite an honor getting into a Masonic home," said Aunt Lou belligerently, glaring at Ruby. "Furthermore I advise you to marry a Mason yourself, young lady, if you want to look out for your old age. Unless it's too late already."

"Is that Corinne's daughter?" Allan asked hastily, as a blond, toothy young girl came hurrying up to him.

"Uncle Allan, why didn't you let us know you were coming?" she cried, throwing her arms around him. "I'm your namesake, Allane, remember?"

"Charlie's youngest," explained Ruby. "Married already, and going to have a baby and only eighteen. Isn't it awful?"

"I had my first baby when I was eighteen," said Aunt Lou, the bird on her hat nodding tremulous confirmation. "Nothing to fuss about. I had my fourth under my belt and had buried two husbands when I was Ruby's age."

"Thirty-one," said Ruby.

"Thirty-two," said Aunt Lou firmly, the bird agreeing. "I was there. Four-fifteen of a Sunday morning, thirty-two years ago July tenth."

"Did you get my wedding invitation?" Allane asked, clinging to Allan's arm. He remembered the faithful chain of Christmas and birthday cards signed "Your loving niece and namesake, Allane" forwarded to him wherever he went, for years and years, in the obvious and pathetic hope of inheriting. Where in God's name was Corinne, he wondered, accepting a sandwich from a passing tray, wishing he could find a drink, but recollecting that this was an ice-cream-and-cake family. He saw Stan's brother, the fat one in real estate, who used to do imitations at all the school parties, pushing toward him through the chattering crowd. In the sea of strangers and vaguely remembered kin it cheered him to get a warm handshake from a contemporary.

"You just missed the Mayor," Dave said in a confidential undertone. "Too bad. I'd have been glad to introduce you, he's not at all stuck-up. But come in and meet the Carpenters, he's president of Stan's company. Came in person. Stan had no idea he'd show up. I'll find him."

"I just came to see Corinne," Allan said.

"Well, the Mayor's quite a character, I guess he's as well known right there in New York City as he is here," Dave replied. "Mayor Green, you know. Made a fortune with his Green Gardens, specializes in glads. You've heard the radio program, of course. 'Gladden your Garden with Green Garden Glads.' Those are his glads in the next room. I'll bet he'd charge five hundred dollars for that work ordinarily. Ever see anything like it?"

"No, I never did," Allan answered truthfully, for he now realized that what had seemed from a distance an aggressive wallpaper was in actuality an entire tapestry of flame-colored gladiolas arranged on vines and moss stretching from ceiling to floor across the whole dining-room wall. The flowers were larger than any Allan had ever seen and he thought that any minute they might lift their heads and turn out to be Rockettes about to execute a Radio City stage number.

"Stan just about cried when the men brought it in yesterday and put it up," Dave said. "It's something to have Mayor Green going out of his way for you. Look, I had a hunch you might come out for this, Allan, and I brought a thing I wrote, it's an idea for a movie. I thought you being married to a movie actress and living in New York you'd know how to go about these things. Of course I'd cut you in for half."

"Betsy and I are divorced," Allan said. "I'm afraid I wouldn't be any help on a movie. Look, where's Corinne? I just want to see her a minute then start driving so I get to Des Moines by morning."

Stan was waving to him from the other room so he pushed through the crowd to him. As he greeted him, Allan saw that he was holding what appeared to be a set of dentures in his left hand.

"Seen the glads, Allan? Cost anybody else a thousand bucks but Mayor Green let me have it as a personal favor. You know our old neighbors here, Doc Filbert, and your cousin Tracy, he flew all the way from Cleveland, and here's Ed. I was just showing Doc here a thousand-dollar job I had done on my teeth lately. I got it for seven hundred as a personal favor, but it would cost anybody else a thousand."

Dr. Filbert, a round bald little man in a very new, very blue suit, accepted the dental specimens from Stan and studied them carefully.

"Standard three-hundred-dollar job," he stated briefly. "You were clipped. Look. Let me show you a genuine thousand-dollar job. Ed, show them what I did for you last summer."

Ed, a tall sandy man with a carnation in his lapel, obligingly removed all his teeth and laid them in Stan's hand.

"I can't understand it," Stan said, shaking his head sadly. "I've done a lot of things in the building line for this dentist of mine, and it ends up with him clipping me. How are you, Allan?"

"I've still got my teeth." Allan replied. "Where's Corinne?"

"I'll take you to her," Stan said, leading him forward. "Just beyond the glads there. You saw them. Mayor Green sent them. Oh, yes, I told you. What the hell does Doc Filbert know about first-class teeth work? He's a hick dentist, never saw more than a thousand bucks in his whole life, probably. Ever see such a mob? Half of 'em showing up just so I'll throw a little business their way, but they got another guess coming, I don't need money that bad. This used to be the boys' room in this wing, not that they ever come home anymore for any length of time. How come you never had any kids, Allan?"

"I guess I thought there were enough Bateses," Allan said.

He was sure Stan would tell him how much the rugs, wallpaper, furniture, and fixtures had cost, how much more they would have cost someone else without his pull, and then would come the inevitable question of how much money *he* was making. It occurred to Allan, already dreading the moment, that such talk seemed either boring or even funny when he was in the chips, but when he was going through a private financial depression it became downright outrageous.

"What about you, Allan?" Stan was already started on it. "Are you doing all right now? Corinne was telling me something about you. Take a lot of trips to the old country, don't you?"

"I—" Allan began, when suddenly Stan pushed against the mossy wall of gladiolas and a door swung open into a large darkened room with a handsome canopy bed in the alcove. A little gray-haired man in a neat gray suit was standing on a chair in the window bay adjusting the tightly drawn shades, but there was no one else around. The daylight was cut out completely, and light came from white candles in glittering candelabra on the mantelpiece, dressing table, and bureau.

"Where's Corinne?" Allan asked, and then he saw her. She looked lovely, as lovely as he remembered her from twenty years ago, long and slender still in the cream satin dress, her hair still shining blue-black, the incredible lashes shimmering like spider legs on the ivory skin, the long narrow hands folded over a prayer book. But her mouth looked tired and drawn, and she seemed like a girl who had passed out quite sweetly in the middle of a long party, though the guests still clamored for her, and would not ever go.

"She looks lovely," Allan said. "It's not Corinne without the old blazing blue eyes, but she does look beautiful."

Stan stood at the foot of the bed in the alcove looking down at his wife with yearning or pride, Allan was not sure which. He wanted to say something but it was hard to know what to say to a man like Stan.

"A lot of the folks criticized me for not having her out under the gladiola wall in the dining room," Stan said. "But I figured she'd like it better in here, all quiet, away from everything, as if she was resting. And in here you can shut out the daylight so it doesn't show up so much when she turns green. See, this is the third day of the lying-in-state. With all my business connections I had to keep her that long. Mr. Jones, will you touch up that right cheek?"

The little old man arranged his curtains and stepped down quickly; leaning over Corinne he whipped out a large compact of pancake makeup and delicately applied it with his two fingers to her right cheek. He stood back a moment, frowning, then produced a lipstick to repair the lips. It reminded Allan that the last time he had seen Corinne was at the senior prom when they had sneaked away from their partners for a farewell ride out to the Grotto and she had cried off her makeup on his shoulder. He remembered tilting the car mirror so she could fix her mouth before she went back into the ballroom to Stan and for years after he dreamed of the shadowy reflection with the bright red lips. Allan had stayed outside in the shadows, ignoring the Whitman girl who was calling his name, straining his eyes to follow Corinne dancing, his heart leaping as he saw her own eyes searching the darkness for him whenever she passed the window. No one knew all that had been between them and that this night had to be the end. Why, she had wept in his arms at their hidden Grotto, why good-bye, and why forever? How many times afterward he had wondered the same, asking himself if youthful wisdom was not more dangerous than youthful folly. The cold painted lips seemed to part and again he heard the whisper Why, why good-bye, and why forever. He caught his breath, afraid that he was going to burst out bawling, with Stan there looking at him.

"I was just thinking what a pity she couldn't see those glads," Allan said in a queer choked voice. "Now she'll never know."

Adam

*W*HEN HE THOUGHT OF where he would be three hours from now it made the little hotel room seem all the more unbearable. It had been a sweltering night and now, with the sun high, the tarred roof below his window wafted melting fumes up to him. Very different, he reflected bitterly, from the cool sea breezes now caressing his darling. Very different, indeed, this dingy room, from the great house at the shore where Mark Burbage took his ease.

Some fellows might work up a real grudge about this, but Adam was too good-natured. Maybe he flared up once in a while, but life was too short. Enjoy what you can and don't worry, that was his motto. In a little while he would be sailing with Virginia, sailing or maybe canoeing, or lounging around the swimming pool with a highball, the dogs tumbling about, good-looking people from other houses laughing and having a good time. Old Burbage, in his shorts and some new fantastic beach robe, lying back in his chair with his eyes closed, not saying much but taking in every little thing. Adam wondered how much he guessed about Virginia and himself.

Burbage was a smooth chap, courteous to everyone, silent but entertained by others' talk. Virginia had hysterical spells sometimes, saying that living with Burbage was like living with a clam; a considerate clam, true, but a clam. Adam didn't see how a gay, high-spirited girl like Virginia had stood it so long. They quarreled because she did stand it, deeply in love with Adam though she was.

Adam looked at his watch. Noon. He was almost packed. The Harolds (Bob Harold was a business partner of Burbage's) were going out for the weekend, too, and were stopping by to pick him up at half past twelve. He was glad he had invested in new luggage, glad the Burbage friends had taken to him, glad, sometimes, of the war that had made it possible for him to meet Virginia and enter a hitherto unknown world.

He remembered the new beach robe he had bought, a worthy rival to Burbage's, and he took it out of the bag again to examine it. He still had to laugh at himself for the first weekend at Virginia's two years ago, when he'd frantically bought a whole new outfit and the servant had mixed up all the guest's belongings.

"Would you mind describing the contents of your bag?" the man had apologetically asked him, but Adam for the life of him could not remember what he had purchased. Finally, in a fit of grim candor he had said, "Why, yes. Mine will be the ones with the price tags still on them."

Now he carefully removed the price tag from the beach robe, a little appalled at the extravagance of the purchase. Fifty-five dollars for what might be used for only two or three weekends. To make it seem reasonable he had told himself that he might be going to Florida next winter. Virginia had said she simply could not endure another season down there without him, and even Burbage had casually suggested that Adam spend a few days with them if he should be going south. Burbage was remarkably decent in ways like that. If he did know what was going on, he saw no cause for rudeness or disagreeable attitudes. Adam wondered if he would have had the guts to go on being crazy about Virginia if there had been any fireworks about it. He hated anything unpleasant, and he hated to have anyone dislike him. In the office they said that was the trait that made him a good salesman.

The telephone rang. He hastily thrust the robe into the bag and shut it, so that he could say he was on his way down rather than have the Harolds see his room.

It was not the desk. It was Virginia.

"Darling, guess where I am!" She sounded breathless.

"In bed, probably," he said.

"I'm in town, Adam," she said. "Listen."

He could hear the sound of church bells bonging over the phone. "Now do you know where I am?" she asked.

"You're not at Della's?" he said incredulously. Della's apartment was near St. Thomas's. "You can't be serious."

"I am. If you come over right away I'll give you lunch."

"But the Harolds are stopping to take me out to your place," he protested, utterly baffled.

"Darling, I'm telling you I am not there. I am here. Here at Della's bag and baggage, with two electric fans going and Della sitting in a cold bath. Aren't you glad?"

He was mystified and more than a little uneasy.

"I'm glad about the cold bath," he said. "Listen, what on earth are you doing in town in this ungodly heat?"

"Is it hot? Is it cold?" Virginia laughed shortly. "Whatever it is I'm here for a long time, darling. Della's letting me stay with her until I get my plans made."

"Why stay with Della?" he asked stupidly.

"She's your friend, dear. She's been wonderful to me. She thinks I've done exactly right and doesn't know why I haven't done it before. She—"

"Done what?" shouted Adam.

"I've left Mark. I couldn't stand it another minute. I stayed at the inn last night and took the first train in. Darling, I'm free! Or I will be when my lawyer fixes it."

It seemed to Adam that the hot breeze from the tar roof carried some anesthetic with it, for he seemed to be falling through space, gasping for air.

"Do you love me, Adam?" Virginia's voice sounded frightened. "I wish you'd come up here and talk things over. I'm terribly upset and scared."

"I can't right now," he said, thinking of the stuffiness of Della's little place on a summer day, the drinking companions dropping in at all hours, everybody chipping in to send out for another bottle, the ice running out, the party moving over to the Third Avenue bars long after midnight. That was his old life, the life he had been so relieved to abandon for Virginia's. What perverse fate had made Virginia pick up that strand? Virginia was delicate, silken, rare, or at least she was against her proper background, the little fairy princess in the big house. He could not think of her apart from that life. He could not think of her in Della's haphazard footless crowd—nobodies; cheerful, idle nobodies. He shuddered and felt a wave of anger at her for stealing something from him, handing the peddler back his rags after the dream was over. "Is Mark still at the shore?" he asked. "What does he say?"

"He doesn't know yet. I had just been going crazy thinking the whole mess over, thinking what was fair to you and what was fair to me and to Mark, too. Then I made up my mind yesterday. I simply couldn't have it out with him face to face, so I ran away—said I had to come in. My lawyer can write him the whole story. Do you blame me for being such a coward, darling?"

"No. No, of course not," Adam said slowly.

He thought she might have waited till the weekend was over at least. It was selfish of her to think only of her own hysterical emotions. Burbage would have thought of everyone else first, keeping the whole matter under control, no one inconvenienced, no one left to swelter in a muggy hotel room when he might be plunging in cool waves with a long cool drink waiting on the terrace. Virginia didn't think of anyone else's pleasure because she had always had her own looked after so thoughtfully. She might be just crazy enough to be fed up with luxury and the rules for gracious living; she might think roistering around with Della was pleasure! Adam thought of the new robe, the trip to Palm Beach nipped in the bud.

"Della says if you come over to bring some fizzywater," Virginia said a little hesitantly. "I know it's sudden, Adam, and I've told you so often the reasons I never could leave Mark, but I just gave up and the reasons just disappeared. You do understand, dear. I didn't want to raise any false hopes before, that was all."

That was sweet of her, he thought! *Wasn't* that sweet of her! Never a word of warning that this might happen. Never any hint that he should take care. False hopes!

There was a knock at the door. He called, "Come in."

"Mr. and Mrs. Harold are downstairs," said the elevator boy. "They're waiting in the car. Is this the bag?"

"Yes," said Adam, as the boy picked it up. He spoke into the phone again. "Virginia, I'm too disturbed about this to talk now. Someone is here. Let me call you again."

"You think it was all right for me to leave Mark?" she was urgently demanding. "I don't care what anyone says; that's what I'm doing."

"You know best, dear," he said and hung up.

In the elevator he gave the boy a coin. "Take a couple of bottles of club soda over to Miss Carter at the Clarendale Apartments with my regards," he said.

Virginia might be leaving Mark, but Adam wasn't.

Day After Tomorrow

$\mathcal{W}$HEN THEY FOUND OUT Lucille was engaged
the girls insisted on a celebration. What about tonight?

"But it'll be months!" Lucille protested. "There's no hurry, really. Besides, I have Mrs. Brady at five and it'll keep me late."

"I'll do the Brady," said Smitty, the big girl, firmly. "We haven't had a shop party for ages. We'll get Frankie to shut up early."

"Better take your party when you can get it," advised Miss Olsen. "When it gets near the wedding day we may be too busy."

Olsen sat at the cashier's desk, under the drier, which shone like a crown above her radiantly fresh facial. Her eyebrows above the porcelain-tinted face were harried to meager wisps like Smitty's and the other girls; but where Smitty's mouth was sullen, Olsen's was large and good-humored. It was Oley who kept the girls from quarreling and getting on Frankie's nerves. You had to have someone like Oley in a beauty parlor. She made Lucille feel that the party was really a business proposition, something a new girl in the trade had to do. Her reassuring, steady eyes followed Lucille over to the telephone.

Mac was sore when Lucille told him she wouldn't meet him tonight. He was jealous enough of the shop, anyway, especially since she made more money there than he did. He was always saying that she was to stop work when they got married but they both knew she couldn't. Most of the girls in Frankie's were married and had never quit their jobs. Lucille had not set a date for the wedding but once in a long while she and Mac would talk about going down to City Hall day after tomorrow. At the last minute something always stopped them, but that was the way it would happen, they both said, one of these days they'd go through with it.

"O.K.?" Oley asked when Lucille left the phone, frowning.

The new girl tried to smile.

"Kinda sulky," she confessed. "I told him it was all right, no men going, not even Frankie, but he hung up on me."

"That's my Albert, too," exclaimed Smitty. "Us girls celebrate about one night a year and you'd think it was every night in the week."

"Your four o'clock is here, Miss Schmidt," shouted Miss Olsen, and suddenly the shop was busy again, the way it always was at the last minute, especially if the girls had something planned. It was as if women didn't know they could get three treatments for five dollars at the shop across the street, it was as if they just had to come to Frankie's and pay double, because he was a great artist. Even above the driers roaring and the canaries singing you could hear Frankie telling everybody what a great artist he was. Smitty winked at the new girl but the new girl believed every word he said.

"He really is a genius," she whispered to the customer whose roots she was touching up. "It's a privilege to study hair work under Frankie, I mean that."

"I even made my own toupee," Frankie was now declaiming, curling iron in hand, in the center of the shop. He had a large pasty pink head adorned by a lavishly curled wig to which he was pointing. "Every place I go people admire that toupee. On the trains, on the street, everywhere. All the time they come up to me, strangers, old, young, everybody. 'Pardon me, sir,' they say, 'that is a beautiful toupee you are wearing. I couldn't help noticing it,' 'Allow me,' they say, 'it's an exquisite piece of work.'"

"Oh it is, Frankie, it is," Lucille eagerly seconded him.

Frankie looked at her approvingly. The new girl was doing all right. Nobody needed to worry about her getting along.

"Frankie thinks you've got a future here," Miss Olsen said to Lucille quietly, when the customer had paid her check. "It's a pity you got other plans."

The new girl was so much younger than the others, so delighted with praise and so eager for advice that you couldn't be jealous of her.

"Oh, but I'll be here a long time anyway," she said happily.

She was thrilled that the older girls wanted to celebrate for her but as night approached she worried more and more about Mac. He was low enough lately, anyway, with work so uncertain.

"What does he do, anyway?" Smitty asked, when she explained her qualms. "Or has he got a job?"

"He does special jobs for a radio firm," Lucille evaded. "Naturally high-class technical jobs don't come every day so— But after Election it will be different, of course."

"And why?" Smitty asked.

"Well," Lucille answered, "because Mac said so."

"Then wait till after Election to get married," counseled Smitty. "Notice if it's different, like he says. Until then pay no attention to what he says about your going on parties."

At six there was a lull in the shop. Mrs. Brady, a weekly problem, all curled, tweezed, tinted, and rouged by Smitty, tottered out on high spike heels, balancing a tower of flowers and birds on her new coiffure, her fat little blond chow tucked under her fat little arm. In a twinkling Smitty had jerked down the window shades, barred the door, slammed the appointment book shut. Marie and Freda, the two blonds, whisked bottles and work trays into lockers, the colored boy started sweeping up hair, and old Mrs. Sweeney dragged in her mop and pail. The fresh smell of suds and disinfectant was a pleasure after the clashing perfumes of the day. Under the black coverlets thrown over their cages the canaries twittered sleepily. Frankie did not object to the early closing because it was his night for *Aida*. In pearl-gray topcoat and soft green hat he stood in the salesroom paring his nails and humming lightly, waiting to lock up. Miss Olsen, who was always the first to be ready, passed the time by calling up her friend Helmar to say she would not meet him at the movie tonight, at all. A girl in the shop was going to be married, she said. She did the other girls the favor of calling husbands to say the shop was keeping the staff late tonight.

"Oley is the smart one," Smitty sighed to the new girl. "You don't catch her getting married."

"Listen," answered Miss Olsen complacently adjusting her veil. "If I do all the work why shouldn't I spend the money on my own comfort instead of on some man? I like a twelve-dollar shoe."

"Oley can go out every week like this," grumbled Smitty. "It's only once a year for us married ones, isn't that so, Freda? Well, where do we go first?"

"Have a good time, girls," said Frankie, as they rushed out. "Don't forget tomorrow morning at eight sharp."

They went across the street to the hotel bar first and sat on stools while the bartender kidded them. They were five good-looking, well-dressed girls. They knew what to wear and where to get it cheap. After two old-fashioneds they were comparing complaints about their husbands. The three married ones had all rowed with their husbands about going out tonight, but they didn't care, they had a right to go out with girls for some fun once a year. A person got tired of going out with a husband every minute, you wanted a good time for a change. Marie and Freda stuck together, whispering secrets, so Lucille stuck to Smitty and Oley.

"Listen, you're a darn fool for getting married," Miss Olsen advised the new girl. "The way I look at it is this. Wouldn't you rather buy one good ticket to Radio City than two to some lousy neighborhood movie? That's the question a girl should ask herself before she takes on a husband."

"It's the truth," said Smitty. "You know how it is. Either a man can't get a job or if he can it don't suit him and he don't make much. You're better off like Oley here, giving the boyfriend a nice present at Christmas, say a good watch or a swell dressing gown. That's the way I see it."

Two traveling men were trying to horn in on the party so they decided to get going.

"We always end up in Greenwich Village," said Smitty. "Boy, oh boy. But don't tell your boyfriend. Come on, kids, here's a taxi."

They stopped at three other bars on the way down, whenever they saw a place that looked gay. Smitty could drink like a trooper but after a few drinks Miss Olsen got her sentences mixed up and finally stopped saying anything but "Hooray for me!" Lucille got the giggles and swore she never had so much fun in her life. She felt guilty having so much fun without Mac and suggested calling him up. He might come down.

"Not a chance," said Smitty. "We don't want any men along."

By the time they got down to Sheridan Square they had had about five old-fashioneds apiece and no dinner. No matter where they went they took a taxi, even if they were only going a block. Marie got to crying because she said before she was married she used to take taxis every day and now it was about twice a year.

The mascara kept running down her cheeks and Freda kept swabbing off her friend's face and trying to make her up again, but Marie would cry it right off again. Everyone was borrowing from Oley by this time, because she always carried money, and besides she could take it right out of their envelopes on Saturday.

"Albert will just have to wait another week for his suit," said Smitty, two dollars in the red. "We were to make a last payment on it this payday. He'll be raving. You know. A man has to look just so when he's not working or he gets low in his mind."

"Wait till he's working!" Marie sniveled. "Then all the money goes for cleaning and pressing and shoeshines. The wife has to pay the rent and gas and bread and cook the beefsteak for his boss."

"I guess it depends a lot on the fella," said Lucille.

"Hooray for me," said Miss Olsen, and then they were at the Joint. The Joint was a long barroom lit up with blue lights, crowded with shouting drinkers and funny-looking Villagers. A jukebox was blaring out "I'm in Love With a Wonderful Guy" so Smitty grabbed Lucille and they danced, falling into the booth at last over Oley's knees and screaming with laughter.

"Dancing," said Marie, "that's another thing I miss."

A boy with a drawing pad came up and wanted to do their portraits for a dollar and Oley consented. She took off her glasses and held her square handsome ruddy face turned to the right for twenty minutes while the waiter brought their hamburgers and beer. The girls wanted to kid the artist because he was a good-looking lad. They could hardly eat for staring at him.

"Look at the complexion on him!" marveled Marie. "Mrs. Brady would give a million dollars for a skin like that."

"It's just the shade of our *rose foncé,*" murmured Smitty. "And look at how he wears his clothes. Boy, it would be a pleasure to dress a fella like that, you could dress him straight from Student Wear and he'd look custom-made."

"He could walk right out of the store without an alteration," said Freda.

"It's when they got a pot like Bill that clothes cost so much," said Marie. "It's a case of skimping over the stomach or else the behind. His new forty-dollar gabardine cuts him right through the middle."

"Tell him to lay off the starches," said Freda.

Oley gave the boy a dollar for her portrait. There was real talent there, she said, and it made her look like Ingrid Bergman, some. But the other girls just kept staring at the artist, as he walked away.

"The way he walks, even," said Smitty dreamily. "You could take a fella like that anywhere and have people take notice. Look at the wave. Frankie ought to see that. The manicure, even. I could look at a fella like that all day and never get tired. If he was mine I'd get him evening clothes, top hat, the whole works."

"And those eyelashes!" said Marie. "Still and all he looks kinda weak."

"I suppose you prefer a prizefighter type," sneered Smitty. "Listen, if you got to have a husband, give me one that shows off what I put into 'em, that's all I say. All Albert can do with his clothes is to look warm."

Lucille was beginning to get serious. She thought of Mac and how the girls would kid about a heavy solid baldish fellow like that with no steady job, no sex appeal, just a fellow you liked. She was worried too, as it got toward eleven, because Mac might take it into his head to drop by her place, checking up on her. She timidly reminded Smitty that it took nearly an hour to get up to 181st Street.

"Listen to the sissy," jeered Marie. "Afraid of the boyfriend, eh? Let him beef. You'll get used to it, honey. Ask him who it is that pays the bills, that's what to say when they get to beefing."

"I got nothing on my mind," boasted Oley. "If Helmar don't like what I do he can take a powder. I got other men friends."

She rolled up her portrait carefully.

"You don't know how smart you are, Oley," said Marie.

"Hooray," said Oley. "Hooray for me."

"That boy!" Smitty said. "Did you see his teeth? I'll bet his dentist bill don't run five dollars a year."

"Forget it!" said Oley. "This party's for Lucille, here, not for that Village sheik."

"That's right," said Smitty, and raised her glass. "To the bride!"

They finished off their glasses but Lucille didn't drink because you didn't drink when it was a toast to you and besides she was getting a queer feeling.

"What say we go?" said Oley. "You kids pay me Saturday."

The jukebox played "Anniversary Waltz" and Freda and Lucille started dancing their way out. The girls were calling Lucille "Baby" now because they said she didn't know the first thing. Outside the air was chilly for June and everyone envied Oley her foxes, even though she said they were only half paid for. They took the subway up to Times Square where Oley and the two blonds changed to East Side and Smitty and Lucille took the Broadway Express. On the way up Smitty got to telling off-color jokes till they thought they'd die laughing. At 181st Smitty went west and Lucille hurried east. She was still laughing when she saw Mac in front of her rooming house. He was walking up and down smoking his pipe and she knew he was sore but she was too happy to care. It was like the girls said, you had a right to a good time once a year.

"There was some man," he said, grabbing her arm. He wouldn't let her go inside the vestibule without an argument. "You can't kid me, there was some other man in it. It was Frankie."

"There wasn't any man in it, dopey," she said irritably. "This was just pleasure."

She went in, letting the door slam, not giving him a chance to ask how much of her salary she'd spent, money that should have been saved toward the apartment. While she undressed she got to thinking of Smitty and her husband having that same argument that very minute, probably, and the other girls the same, and she thought only Oley was having a good night's sleep without a care. So far as that went it wasn't too late for her to change her own mind. The wedding date wasn't really set. There was still time to decide on one ticket to Radio City instead of two to a neighborhood movie. When Mac started bawling her out tomorrow she'd have something to say right back.

She climbed into bed with her nightgown on wrong side out. She lay there in the dark watching the blue garage lights go on and off across the street, thinking what a wonderful evening they had had. She thought about Oley's silver foxes and twelve-dollar shoes and the boy with the *rose foncé* complexion.

"Hooray for me!" she shouted suddenly.

She must have been a little tight.

Ideal Home

Eᴌɪᴢᴀʙᴇᴛʜ's ᴇʏᴇs ᴡᴇʀᴇ ʀᴇᴅ again at breakfast. Neither Vera nor her mother said anything about it, but leave it to Lewey to speak up.

"Lose your beau again?" he jeered. "What's the matter you can't hold 'em?"

"Elizabeth's a drip," Vera stated pleasantly.

Elizabeth snatched up her coffee cup and took it into the living room, but that reminded her once more of how hopeless everything was. No privacy, no privacy at all. Kitchen, dinette, and living room all in one. Modern. Ideal. Over the bookcase partition that swung out to mark off the dinette Lewey stared at her critically, stirring his coffee.

"Why'ncha wear that new bathrobe you were saving up for?"

"Hostess gown!"

"Well, why'ncha wear it instead of that faded old rag?"

"Because it's to entertain in, dopey!"

"That's why that goon last night didn't ask her out," Vera observed impassively. "He thought she was ready for bed."

Lewey roared. He thought everything Vera said was a scream. Lewey was twenty, four years older than Elizabeth. He had a girl, Thelma. Thelma worked in the shipping department of the company where Elizabeth was file clerk, and she was forever telling people Lewey was going to marry her next week. Elizabeth wished to God he would, but after all what good would it do to have Lewey out of the apartment? Nine-year-old Jimmy was growing up to be just as mean, and Vera, at only fourteen, made life unbearable with all her boyfriends and the telephone always ringing for her. Fat chance a girl with an unusual personality had in a household like this! What's more, it got worse all the time. It was all on account of the new apartment, and Elizabeth had to admit that she was to blame for that. Oh yes, they must move into the wonderful modernistic Ideal Cooperative Apartment house. A girl with ambition had no chance in an old-fashioned tenement, you read that everywhere. Spacious rooms (two), In-a-door beds, sunlight, air, everything electric, everything glass, just push a button! Well, what was so special about sunlight? What was so wonderful about walls sliding back to make one big room so the whole family could spy on you? At least in the old railroad-style apartment there was a room for everybody, even if it was only closet size. You had a place to cry. At least you had a vestibule downstairs where a girl could have a little privacy entertaining, instead of a big square lobby with fluorescent lights blazing all night like day. Supposing a girl didn't know a fellow, at least she could get kinda acquainted in the old vestibule without the handicap of a spotlight. For that matter the long narrow hall in the old place had been all right, too. A person could come in without stumbling over a trick bed. Elizabeth wished now she had kept her mouth shut, instead of dinging at them all the time to move here and give herself and Vera a chance to live nice. What better use for Papa's insurance money? All right, she argued them into it, so now they were stuck here for life.

"It's the only bright idea Elizabeth ever had," the whole family agreed.

Sure. It had worked out for everybody but herself.

"Why'ncha fix up your eyes?" Lewey suggested. "All those bottles and jars of yours ought to do something for you. Hey, Vera, did you see that new stuff Liz's got? Marbe's Elbow Cream, I'm not kidding! Ha!"

Elizabeth's mouth set. A girl worked and studied to make something of herself and train her personality like those books said, and all you got was your family making fun of you, laughing at you in front of your company whenever you were trying to have an intelligent conversation. What good was it to be sophisticated and keep your elbows bleached and your skin stimulated if you never had a chance to show off? Even in the office, when she was having a little intelligent conversation with Mr. Ross, the personnel chief, there was always Thelma grinning, ready to blab whatever she said to the family.

"Where'd you dig up that mug last night? Never opened his trap." Lewey always had to rub it in.

"Why would he with the whole darn family peeking over at him?" Elizabeth retorted bitterly.

"Ah, you're all right, old girl, don't get sore," Lewey yawned. He plucked the newspaper out of Vera's hands and made for the big chair in the corner. "Trouble is, you don't know what time it is. Your feet's too big."

There was a thudding noise in the next room. That would be the beds folding up into bookcases. The creaking sound that followed was Vera's bed turning over into a refectory table. Now the master bedroom was a library, the bookshelves adorned anew with Vera's china animals, Jimmy's comics, a handpainted tray, two World's Fair plates, and a set of Kipling. Mrs. Neeley, rosy-faced from effecting this routine transformation, came out with a towel pinned around her head and a dustcloth in her hand.

"That was one of the boys you met at camp, wasn't it, Elizabeth?" she asked. "He got out so fast I didn't get a chance to talk to him."

"It's the one she wrote about in her diary," Vera said, now industriously painting her nails. "He's a drip."

Her diary! Elizabeth ran into the kitchenette, put her cup and saucer in the sink, and let the noise of running water do its best to cover her gulping sobs. If only there was a door to slam, a key to lock, in the darn new Ideal Home! The only place she had to hide her secrets was the desk drawer in her office and what use was that weekends?

"Is that the one, dear?" her mother asked. She poured furniture oil on her dustcloth and applied it to the desk. "Would you believe it, I can clean this place top to bottom in an hour? You know how long it took in the old place. I can't get over it."

In the mirror above the kitchen sink Elizabeth took gloomy pleasure in seeing how pasty and swollen her face looked this morning. She had looked wonderful last night and a lot of good it had done her. In her lunch hour she had had her first facial not in a beauty parlor, but by a lady demonstrator free of charge in the cosmetic department of Hearn's.

"See what this cream does to wrinkles, folks?" the lady demonstrator had shouted, after Elizabeth had volunteered for the free demonstration. A small circle of shoppers stared curiously at the operation. "This young lady is too young for wrinkles, and a little too plump for them to show up anyway, but she has these here lines we call laughter lines. Ladies, you got to watch them laughter lines."

At this rate her face would be riddled with laughter lines before she got a boyfriend, Elizabeth thought. She was sixteen, old enough to "take care of herself" where boys were concerned, her mother said, but where were they? She'd only had three dates since they moved and then the whole family horned in on them. The camp had been different. The camp had been wonderful. If she'd only had more than five days something might have happened.

"At the camp there are these four fellows," she had written in her diary, August 24, "and I hardly know what to do. They laugh and kid at meals, but when it comes to going for a walk they take the other girls like I was poison. But Tuesday night Philip, that's the tall one, he's from Buffalo, New York, took me for a walk. At first I thought he wouldn't but after a while he did kiss me and was just as lovely to me as he could be. He sure looks cute with his new haircut, just like a prisoner of war. . . ."

It turned out that even Mrs. Tully, the janitress, had snooped into her diary, because Elizabeth overheard her saying to her mother, "That book of your daughter's is real interesting. She sure had some good times at that church camp, at least to hear her tell it. This fellow, Philip, he seems quite a character. I guess she makes up a lot in her head, too."

It had taken four letters, all casual and kidding, full of jokes about being the "forgotten woman," to get the postcard from Philip, saying he was going to visit New York and might call her up. Of course, the whole family knew all about it. They even found all the copies of the letters she'd written, and razzed her about them. In desperation Elizabeth had humbled herself to ask Vera where on earth she managed to hide her secrets, only to have the foxy little thing lift dainty eyebrows and say, "I don't hide things. I burn them. Honestly, Liz, you're such a drip!"

Well, Philip had called on her, all right, and this morning there was nothing more to look forward to and nothing to remember, either. Lewey and Thelma had elected last night to stay in playing cards and drinking beer in the dining alcove, keeping an eye on Elizabeth and audibly mocking her company conversation. She had made up her mind to be cultivated instead of up to

date, because the time she had tried to use the expression
"Hubba hubba" Vera had cried out, "Oh, Liz, you never catch
on to anything until it's out of date." Vera was out with her
bunch getting autographs when Philip called, thank goodness,
but the telephone kept ringing for her just to show Philip who
was the beauty of the family. Just once had it rung for Elizabeth
and then it was only Mr. Ross from her office saying he was
working late and wanted to know where she kept the file-room
key. When she told him she carried it with her Mr. Ross said
never mind, but she hung on sort of kidding and giggling to
make Philip think it was another beau. Mrs. Neeley offered to
send out for ice cream and cakes, as if it was some children's
party, and Elizabeth scornfully rejected this, suggesting beer instead; the young man leapt up and said he guessed he'd go take
in a movie before it was too late. Elizabeth followed him out to
the elevator in case he cared to kiss her good night, but the big
lights were brighter than ever and he acted scared to death.
Lewey and Thelma were laughing about his gawkiness almost
before he was out of hearing.

"The only time he opened his head was when he made that
crack about Liz's figure," giggled Thelma. "'I didn't remember
your being so heavy-set, Miss Neeley,' he says. I woulda popped
him if he said that to me, the little squirt."

End of Philip, Elizabeth had thought, and had gone in the
bathroom and cried for half an hour. What she minded most,
she thought this morning, was not being able to think about him
anymore.

"He seemed like a nice little fellow, that boy last night," Mrs.
Neeley called to Elizabeth. "Maybe he'll drop around again today
and you can have the place to yourselves. Maybe he'll take you out."

"I never saw anybody like Liz," Vera remarked dispassion-
ately. "You'd think she never heard of the facts of life. Only one
fellow ever kissed her."

"How do you know?" Elizabeth snapped. "You haven't any conception of what goes on in my life. How would you find out anyway?"

"I read all about it," Vera said. "I read all about it up to the day you took your diary to your office."

"Now stop teasing. Elizabeth's my good girl," Mrs. Neeley admonished soothingly. "I don't know where she gets it but I know I can always depend on my Elizabeth."

"Imagine going to a Sunday School camp at her age!" Vera muttered, lapsing into silence at a warning shake of the finger from her mother.

Lewey threw down the paper, stretched his large frame, and got to his feet.

"Get a move on, Mom. I got the truck in back. Ride you over to the market if you make it snappy."

"Wait a second," Vera said. "you can drop me at the drugstore for my lipstick. If the kids come by tell 'em I'll be back in a flash, Liz."

"Going to be gone all day then?" her mother asked.

Vera pulled a yellow sweater over her scanty little chest, not deigning to answer such a superfluous question. Saturdays Vera always went someplace with her crowd, usually to the beach. She had an even tan over every inch of her small body, a matter of mystification to Elizabeth and pride to her mother. Mrs. Neeley often remarked to neighbors, "Vera got her mind set on getting an even tan all over and she just stuck to it till she got it. I never realized the kid had that much gumption."

"Elizabeth will be in if Jimmy gets in from the country today," Mrs. Neeley said, picking up her market bag and hurrying after Lewey. "I wouldn't want him to come home to an empty apartment."

"What makes you so sure I'm not going out?" Elizabeth demanded sulkily, but the banging of the outer door was her only answer.

Now that it was of no use to her Elizabeth had the whole apartment to herself. She read the beauty column in the *News* and tried out an ankle exercise it recommended. She did her hair over in a crooked new hairdo she saw pictured and felt cheered to read that hips were coming back. She had almost forgotten her recent woe when the doorbell rang. Her first thought was that maybe Philip was really dropping in, just as her mother had prophesied. But it was Mr. Ross, a slight little man with a crumpled raincoat over his arm and a worn briefcase in hand, who stood at the door.

"I saw you weren't far from where I live so I thought I'd drop by for your key," he explained. "I've got a lot of work to clean up over the weekend and I'll need the files. Say, this is a fine place you've got here."

Elizabeth's disgust with the Ideal Apartment gave way at once to a proud demonstration of sliding walls, magic beds, and windows changing into walls. Mr. Ross's astonishment made her boast that it was she who had first heard about the building and insisted on her family moving there even though it was a queer neighborhood, all warehouses around.

"I guess you're the kind that keeps up on everything," Mr. Ross said. "I got that impression first time I talked to you at the office. By the way, Miss Neeley, another thing. Here's a piece of your property I found out on your desk."

He pulled a small red leather volume from his pocket and Elizabeth saw with a sinking sensation that it was her diary.

"I didn't open it," Mr. Ross said, "naturally."

"That was nice of you," Elizabeth said faintly, and then added in a rush of relief, "How awful if any of the office kids had found it! Oh, how lucky you had to work late! I mean—excuse me, I mean lucky for me. I'm sure it's no fun for you working all weekend."

Mr. Ross seemed to be in no hurry to go to his work, for he sat down on the sofa and lit a cigarette.

"I don't know," he said somberly. "Sometimes you'd rather be in an office working than home worrying over family troubles. That's the case with me, anyway."

Elizabeth was uncertain what to say so she studiously examined her thumbnail. She remembered Mr. Ross had a wife and two children who had called at the office one day. Mrs. Ross was a thin little blond with bulging blue eyes and matchstick legs, but with roses and streamers on her hat as if she thought she was pretty, or else somebody else thought so. Mr. Ross was a frail little man, too, with deep-set and dark eyes and neat boyish features. He must be close to thirty, Elizabeth thought, not really old, but his gloomy expression made him seem so.

"I must apologize for calling up so late last night," he said. "I hope you hadn't gone to bed."

"Mercy no," Elizabeth laughed airily. "I was just about to go out with a boyfriend of mine from Buffalo, New York."

"Serious?" inquired Mr. Ross politely.

Elizabeth shrugged her shoulders.

"I don't know how he feels but it's certainly not serious with me," she said lightly. "He's too slow for me."

"I guess that's my trouble," Mr. Ross said, staring at the carpet. "Yes, that's just about the way my wife sizes me up. Frankly, that's why I go to the office weekends. When I'm home around my wife I got so much on my mind I just about go crazy, but never mind. A young lady like you doesn't want to be bothered with serious problems. No time for it."

"Why Mr. Ross, please!" Elizabeth protested. "You know I always have time for a little intelligent conversation. I have problems, too."

"I know," said Mr. Ross, and Elizabeth looked at him suspiciously, wondering if he had read her diary, after all, but he evidently meant something else for he went on, "You're the sympathetic type. Last night when you were so friendly to me over the telephone I got the idea that maybe you'd be just the person to talk to. Nothing personal, understand. Just take a situation. What would you think, for instance, if every time the phone rings your wife jumps for it and says something you can't make out, then says she has to go out to the grocery store and runs out, comes back in an hour or so without any packages? What would you think of a situation like that, Miss Neeley?"

"Why, I wouldn't think anything," Elizabeth answered, uncertain of what was expected but flattered to be asked.

Mr. Ross reflected on this for a moment.

"Take another case. Supposing your wife tells you she's going to play bridge with some party and then a couple hours later the party calls up asking for her? Miss Neeley, wouldn't it strike you she was meeting some other man?"

Elizabeth was embarrassed not to have thought of this and made up for her slip by answering lightly, "Well, what if she was?"

Mr. Ross regarded her steadily with his mournful eyes.

"I take it you think it's all right for married woman to run around with other men."

"Married men do," Elizabeth said cautiously, with an uncomfortable feeling of being on unfamiliar ground.

"Some do. Some don't," Mr. Ross said. "However, I see your point. I guess I'm old-fashioned. It's a good thing to get the modern angle."

"There's always two sides to everything," Elizabeth produced from the deeper wells of her mind. "You've got to take things into consideration. We're living in a modern age, Mr. Ross."

Mr. Ross thought about this.

"I suppose that being a modern young lady you think nothing at all about married people having affairs. I suppose I seem to you like an old dodo."

"Oh no, Mr. Ross!" Elizabeth hastened to assure him. "I enjoy talking about serious things. I think it was awfully nice of you to bring my diary, too."

"Nice," Mr. Ross repeated with a short laugh. "That's it. I'm nice when I ought to be up to date. I ought to talk to you more, Miss Neeley, it would do me good. The fact is you've been around. Working all my life the way I have, I've been missing the boat right and left."

"Well, I try to keep aware of what time it is," Elizabeth admitted.

"I guess I'd better be going," said Mr. Ross, but he made no move to rise. "You know I'm sort of surprised about you, Miss Neeley. You always seemed to me so much steadier than the girls around the office. I mean I never see you fooling around with the boys there the way the rest do."

Elizabeth flushed defensively.

"Oh *them!*" she exclaimed scornfully. "They're all drips. I like fellows I can discuss things with."

"I guess you have a lot of fellows," Mr. Ross said thoughtfully. "I suppose you think nothing of kissing and that sort of thing. For instance, take a case of where you might see your wife kissing somebody you wouldn't think anything about it."

Elizabeth laughed gaily.

"Mercy, Mr. Ross, nobody thinks anything of kissing nowadays!"

"I guess that's it," Mr. Ross said.

He got up and studied the floor silently.

"I must try not to be old-fashioned," he said, and with an air of intense determination pulled Elizabeth toward him and kissed her furiously. Elizabeth was so dumbfounded she made no protest. Mr. Ross was not as tall as she was but she was frightened, and the sight of Vera in the door was a great relief. Mr. Ross, his face scarlet and quite overcome by his daring, snatched his briefcase and raincoat and rushed past Vera murmuring some inarticulate phrases.

"Who was that?" Vera demanded accusingly.

"Mr. Ross," Elizabeth gasped.

"I thought he was married," Vera said, her sharp eyes examining her sister curiously. "You told us he was a married man."

"Oh what of it, for goodness sake?" Elizabeth cried out impatiently, wishing she could be alone to puzzle out this strange event.

"He was kissing you," Vera said. "I saw him. A married man."

"What of it, I said?" Elizabeth exclaimed. She supposed Vera would lose no time telling the whole family so they would have something new to tease her about. Maybe she could bribe her.

"I'll wash the dishes tomorrow," she said.

Vera was so long in responding to this offer that Elizabeth stole an uneasy look at her. Her sister seemed to be frozen in the doorway, her head cocked to one side, her eyes fixed on her with an expression Elizabeth could not fathom at once, never having encountered it before. There was cool appraisal, as usual, but admiration as well.

"You don't need to," said Vera and added enigmatically, "Maybe I'll do my hair that way, too."

Blue Hyacinths

There was no reason in the world why the two women should not have made excellent friends. They were both resigned to futures without men—Miss MacBane as spinster, Mrs. Delcart as widow. They were both irretrievably lost somewhere in the forties; they were both intense observers of life, waiting rapaciously for it to creep out of its hole. True, their angles were slightly different in so far as either one stands still and observes matter shooting past, or shoots past oneself and observes stationary objects. Miss MacBane had up to this time stood still; Mrs. Delcart had up to this moment shot past. They met as they were both changing their minds in Stateroom 654 of the S.S. *Barnabetta*— Miss MacBane's first voyage, Mrs. Delcart's avowed last.

Mrs. Delcart, as was her custom, had spent the first few hours on deck examining the passengers, chatting with the purser and various ships officials who knew her well as a restless widow who swooped from continent to continent, sometimes with a

dachshund, sometimes with an adopted Turkish orphan, sometimes with a great bunch of Easter lilies, and occasionally with
the merest volume of verse, all depending on where she'd been.
She had sent cables to the friends who had so gladly seen her off,
and had sat for a while in the lounge with a fixed sociable smile
that fooled nobody.

It was invariably at this point, as the lost shore was drifting
away softly into the distance like a vagabond glacier and the ship
definitely committed to some opposite goal, that Mrs. Delcart
had a momentary *crise*. Why had she left the West, why was she
traveling east (or vice versa)—and why Mallorca or Mexico or
the Bahamas of all places? Never could she honestly say it was
because she liked to travel for she'd never had time between trips
to think out exactly what she did like; certainly she hated all the
countries that had ever served her as destination as much as she'd
ever disliked her homeland. It was more than probable that Mrs.
Delcart was one of those people who travel out of sheer nervous-
ness when it would be far better for all concerned if they just
stayed at home and twitched.

Such a conclusion had finally come to Mrs. Delcart herself.

Why, she asked herself as she wrote a letter saying something
totally different to a bridge acquaintance in Nice, why should I, a
woman of years, be an exile in every land, forgotten as soon as I
leave a hotel, remembered only for my patronage, spending my
life dining with casual strangers, my deepest affections mere
gratitude to a good bridge partner? How much more satisfying,
in sum, to take a suite at the Peter Stuyvesant on a forty-year
lease and really live sanely, safely rooted, protected, respected,
and who knows in time so familiar a figure as to be loved by all
out of sheer desperation? Convinced that she was making a final
decision, Mrs. Delcart, with her bright smile all arranged in case
someone might think she did not remember him or her from
their lovely trip through Portugal once, descended to her state-

room to find Miss MacBane prostrated in her bunk as indeed she had been ever since the anchor had been lifted and the ship in motion. Mrs. Delcart's face hardened at the sight. For one thing she had distinctly requested that she have a stateroom to herself no matter how crowded the boat might be, and while no one had ever paid the slightest attention to her requests heretofore, the present defection made her quite as angry as if it were the first time that she, a spoiled darling of the steamship companies, had ever been defied.

"So you're going to be sick," she said.

Miss MacBane managed a pallid smile and turned her face to the wall. Mrs. Delcart, swathed in resentment of a genteel sort, busily unpacked a small English bag. She hung a padded red silk robe on the door beside Miss MacBane's blue merino as if "everyone should wear padded red silk robes!" She took out a wooden guest toothbrush and brushed her teeth vigorously as if "everyone should brush their teeth when traveling," and Miss Mac-Bane, even with her back turned, now knew that everyone should carry little packets of plain wooden toothbrushes. Mrs. Delcart undressed, removing each article with a statement that she always bought her corsets in London, her lingerie in Italy, her jasmine sachet must be made of the Corsican jasmine, and above all she conveyed to Miss MacBane that no one need be ashamed of her body no matter where it was purchased. Finally, in a slip and a bedjacket, she climbed into bed, Miss MacBane fervently hoped, to read or nap, but it was actually to talk, for Mrs. Delcart had forgiven Miss MacBane's existence now and was prepared to go through the traveler's duty of confiding not only the story of her life and marriage to Major Delcart of Montreal, but even her inmost thoughts including her recent decision to give up the open road.

Miss MacBane, in all frankness, did not want to listen. She wanted to be alone so that she might die sadly but decently of this dreadful disease that had never attacked her in all her quiet years at the Hotel Hinckley. She kept her face to the wall because she hated to look at great hulking women like Mrs. Delcart; herself being the type her companion would have classified as "wizened," she had always felt that anything over a hundred and thirty-five pounds was a horrid display of glandular efficiency. She thought of staggering somehow on deck, but then she would be accosted by that dreadful old man who had told her to eat nothing but chicken sandwiches and celery—such neighborly feeling could always be squashed at the Hinckley but it was obvious that a tourist had no defense.

"I want to feel my THINGS about me," said Mrs. Delcart, her voice choking up ever so slightly, "I'm tired of living in a trunk. I want my own little flat where I can see my own true friends day in and day out, people who care if I'm sick or old, people who can play decent contract or chess and in my own language. I want a harbor, Miss Muldoon, after all my vagabond years I do indeed."

Mrs. Delcart could not remember at the moment the names of more than two or three tried old friends in New York but it seemed to her the city was teeming with their tender, sympathetic faces—the names would come later. Unaware of the cozy dislike she had inspired in Miss MacBane she fancied that even here was a true friend. Perhaps together they could go to little Italian restaurants, to foreign movies, and even to the opera if sufficiently aroused.

"My life has been wasted, Miss Muldoon," she said and blew her nose with unexpected vigour. "The best years, too. Honolulu today—Newfoundland tomorrow. I haven't been fair to myself."

She wanted to know if Miss MacBane could suggest a good permanent hotel near the Park. The simple appeal made the other forget for the moment her present misfortune in a rush of loyal affection for her old hotel. She forgot that only two weeks ago she had wept over fifteen years wasted in a hotel room while mad beautiful things were going on all over the rest of the world; she forgot that it had seemed to her then that if she ever heard the clink of her breakfast tray being set inside her door at 8 A.M. morning after morning she would go absolutely berserk; she forgot how perfectly unendurable the familiar phobias of her three oldest, dearest friends there had become. She only thought of it as Home.

"Go to the Hinckley, Mrs. Elkhart," she said, raising her head from her pillow as if to make a dying request. "You can live there for years without being spoken to by strangers. You can get a room facing the park but the children make so much noise it's much wiser to get one on the court where it's as quiet as the grave. The food isn't fancy but it's plain, good American food and when you don't like the dessert you can always take a bag of oranges to your room. And there are musical evenings—usually chamber music—and the hotel guests can go free of charge. Lectures too and tonight"—and here it was Miss MacBane's turn to shed a very small tear—"there was to be a ballet of *Cynara*. I'm—I'm rather sorry to have missed it."

"It sounds divine," answered Mrs. Delcart and added rather thoughtfully, "simply divine."

"I was a fool to have left it," said Miss MacBane bitterly. "Someone else will get first choice on the next court suite. It isn't just a court, mind you—you can look down and see quite a large-sized hyacinth bed with four—no six little fir trees and a bird bath. I don't know what possessed me to take this awful trip. I thought I needed a change—can you imagine? I'm going to wire Mr. Hinckley this very minute to do what he can to save my old rooms for me."

"I would," said Mrs. Delcart. She was suddenly silent. Rather moodily she surveyed Miss MacBane's slight figure, barely enough of her, thought Mrs. Delcart, to keep the sheets from sticking together. The Hinckley would be full of women like that. Mrs. Delcart thought of the years passing at the Hinckley with no stranger to accost her or lend fresh ears to her anecdotes about the Major; she thought of the quiet graveyard room looking out on a spoonful of pale blue hyacinths; she thought of the skimpy echoes of Thursday night chamber music and she saw a man in black tights princing around pantomiming *Cynara*. She thought of the *World-Telegram* she would buy to hide her bag of oranges from the desk clerk. She thought of being trapped by sickness or senility in the Hinckley with no new stewards to bully, no strangers to whom she could complain, no foreigners to upbraid. Mrs. Delcart suddenly reached in her bag and brought forth a large bottle of brandy.

"Will you have a touch, Miss Muldoon?" she asked. "I never drink but I do sometimes take a little brandy when I'm low."

"Thank you, no," said Miss MacBane, as she rang for the steward. The message, she said, was to go to Mr. Walter Hinckley of the Hotel Hinckley. "Do all you can to reserve Suite 12B for another five-year lease as of August 1, date of my return.... Oh yes, Mrs. Elkhart, shall I say anything about reserving a suite for you? Might as well do it now."

Mrs. Delcart had found an illustrated folder of the Scandinavian line among her papers and was examining it thoughtfully.

"Oh, let it go," she answered.

The Roof

 *N*ow, FATHER, DON'T GET the idea we're putting you out," his daughter-in-law said when she showed him the little room on the roof where he was to stay. "It's just that it's hard for the baby to sleep when you have a coughing spell, and with only the four rooms it's hard on you, too."

"You're too good to me, Agnes," Professor Swenstrom said. "I couldn't ask for anything nicer than this."

There were twenty maids' rooms on the top floor of the big apartment building, but up until the war they were seldom used by the tenants except for storage. The younger domestics didn't like to live that near their employers or that far away from the temptations of a less respectable neighborhood. Then after the war, when rooms were scarce, the little cubbyholes were snatched up for soldier-sons' returns, dependent relatives, and retired servants. There were washrooms at each end of the long hall, and on the outside a narrow brick-walled terrace extended the length of the building. As Agnes pointed out, you could sit there and see the Chrysler Tower and watch the skywriting planes above the hum of the city. It was a world in itself up there, suspended between the blue heaven of tomorrow and the hurly-burly of today.

"Why, I think it's perfectly fine, Agnes," Professor Swenstrom declared, "I can get the sun without ever going down to the street, and I can type or play my radio at night without disturbing anyone."

To tell the truth he was really pleased, for his son's apartment was crowded enough with the new baby, and he was glad of a little privacy and the feeling of not being in anybody's way. He had an electric plate and a window icebox of simple supplies so that he could fix his own snacks, and Agnes brought up dinner for him in the middle of every day. He could hear her firm voice talking to the elevator man first, which gave him a chance to turn on his radio full blast covering up his coughing if he was having a spell that might worry her.

"You and your baseball!" Agnes had exclaimed. "I guess you really enjoy being off to yourself this way, listening to that radio."

Baseball was the best because it made the most noise and sounded so healthy. People might object to it sometimes but he knew they would rather be annoyed by baseball than by the sound of an old man wheezing and snorting. He was still too weak from his long illness to care much about moving around, so he just huddled in his chair in his bathrobe, shuffling down the hall to the bathroom or to pick up the papers his son sent up. Days passed before he even felt up to taking a turn on the terrace. He had heard women's voices often but they seemed to come from far off. When he finally went on the terrace he was surprised to see a tall, gaunt old woman in an old-fashioned Japanese kimono, standing by the brick wall just two windows past his own. She was holding up a potted geranium and at first

Swenstrom thought she must be talking to it for he saw no one else around.

"You know how dead it was but it came back as soon as I used that stuff you sent," she was saying, then she saw him and nodded brightly. "You're our new neighbor, Professor Swenstrom, aren't you, the one with asthma? I've heard you at night and wanted to give you some of my husband's medicine, but then I thought I wouldn't intrude. I'm Mrs. Taylor. My nephew's in 3L."

It embarrassed Swenstrom that even up here he had bothered someone with his complaint. He murmured an apology and then heard another sharp female voice cry out, "Is that our new neighbor, Mrs. Taylor?"

"Meet Professor Swenstrom, Mrs. Coltman," said Mrs. Taylor, and pointed across the brick wall to a window in the back of the building across the fifteen-story chasm. A woman in a dust cap and apron was leaning out and waved gaily to him. Swenstrom bowed, warmed by these friendly overtures. His illness had alienated him from all but doctors, nurses, and the relatives who regarded him as their Christian duty.

"Mrs. Coltman's a Jersey girl," Mrs. Taylor said. "I'm Pennsylvania, so she and I are always arguing about which state has the best cooking. But let me tell you I could never beat Mrs. Coltman's lemon pies. Next time she sends one over you'll have to have a piece, Professor."

"We do things right in Jersey," Mrs. Coltman shouted out shrilly, and added with pride, "Did I tell you I made one for my son last Sunday when he came to visit me? 'No, Mother, you stop spoiling me!' I said right back, 'Nonsense, son, you're the one that's spoiling me fixing me up with a pressure cooker up here!'"

"Her son's apartment's on the first floor over there," Mrs. Taylor explained. "The basements of both houses are joined so she can send something down by her elevator man to our basement and one of our boys brings it up." She raised her voice. "Take care of your heart now, Mrs. Coltman."

She put the geranium down in the corner of the terrace beside some other potted plants, tweaked off a yellow leaf, and beckoned peremptorily to Swenstrom. "Now, Professor, you come right to my room and I'll give you that medicine. As soon as I heard you coughing I knew you needed it. My kettle's on and we'll have a nice cup of tea."

Back in the narrow dark corridor, Mrs. Taylor, limping on a rugged-looking cane required since her fall, as she said, led the way to the room where she had lived for four years. The tiny cell was jammed with ancient photographs, Indian rugs, Mexican masks, travel posters, and other evidences of former solvency and worldliness. Mrs. Taylor lost no time in testifying to as much, at the same time administering to her guest a cup of tea and two soiled gray pills from a small silver snuffbox. Swenstrom saw no way of refusing them, dubious though they appeared.

The pills had been created by a South American Indian when Mrs. Taylor's husband had been taken ill in Bogota, and no one knew what was in them but they were certainly magic, and every time Mr. Taylor had had a bronchial spell or touch of asthma he had resorted to this native remedy. He had died, it seemed, of asthma with bronchial complications, but Mrs. Taylor seemed to be nonetheless confident of the cure. She was warm in her welcome of a new neighbor, for most of the top-floor residents "went below" early every morning, and moved to better quarters so fast she never had a chance to get acquainted. She said it was the same case in Mrs. Coltman's building, so the two ladies had struck up a kind of back-fence friendship out of sheer loneliness. To tell the truth, Mrs. Taylor had never seen any more of Mrs. Coltman than what little the window revealed.

"I wouldn't know her on the street," Mrs. Taylor confided. "I don't know whether she's tall or short. But it's nice having someone nearby, you'll find out if you stay up here."

Mrs. Coltman had gone below last December and done Christmas shopping at Namms, in Brooklyn, but she had brought back from this safari the word that the city had gotten so dirty and crowded she wouldn't leave her roof again till they carried her out. Mrs. Taylor herself never went below anymore, not since she'd fallen on the icy street two years ago. She didn't even go down to her nephew's apartment for Sunday dinner the way she used to do, because it made her feel so bad. It wasn't because it had once been her own apartment and still held her belongings, Mr. Taylor's Mexican guitar, her son's piano (that is, the son lost in the Pacific isles), and the oak desk built by the other son (the one who'd fought in Germany). It wasn't the being reminded that she would never lay eyes on the little granddaughter somewhere in Germany because the son's wife could never be found. It wasn't that she minded having nobody, no one left but her husband's nephew, and him such a dull fellow even for a lawyer, and his wife a complete little ninny. It wasn't that they made her feel in the way or that they were in any respect rude to her; the shoe was in fact on the other foot. She had moved up here of her own free will, and had made it quite clear that she didn't want them bothering about her for she had Clary, her old cook coming in once a week ready to do her errands. No, the reason she felt so bad whenever she went below was something else.

"It's the canary," Mrs. Taylor confessed, pushing her wide sleeves back up a bony arm to pour more hot water from the tiny kettle into Swenstrom's clay cup. "Every time I hear that canary of theirs it reminds me of my troupial bird and I can hardly stand it. You won't believe me, sir, but when my bird went I just went to pieces, and that canary brings it all back, of course."

It was approaching the hour in the afternoon when his chest would begin to act up, and Swenstrom prayed it would keep off today so he wouldn't start wheezing right after his kind new friend had given him the cure.

"I don't think I've ever heard of that bird," he said.

"It's a very, very rare bird," said Mrs. Taylor softly, and she fixed her eyes on Swenstrom's intently as if willing him to see what she was seeing. "The Indian who gave us the pills gave us the bird and we didn't like birds, but this troupial bird was the dearest bird we had ever seen. No bigger than a robin, mind you, yellow with black wings, and those knowing yellow eyes with heavenly-blue skin around them and black feather lashes like a doll, mind you, and how it could sing! Professor Swenstrom, it went straight to your heart, a wild, sweet bugle tone that you could hear above everything else—traffic banging, boat whistles—children crying—Mr. Taylor coming home at night could hear it on his bus two blocks away! Oh how it sang! It was all Mr. Taylor cared about in his last sickness. The boys used to write that they missed Fifi—that's what we called her—more than anything else. When she sang you could see that blue tropical sky and the palms and tall jungle trees and picture her mate singing back to her from far off. When I was alone, finally, I had Fifi's cage beside me wherever I went, and the very day she stopped singing—she went like *that,* just put her little head in my hand and gave up!—that very day I moved up here and gave the apartment to my nephew. That very day! I couldn't stand it. And then when they got a canary thinking it would comfort me—well, you can imagine how much worse I felt."

He could tell the attack was coming on and Swenstrom got up, perspiration beading on his forehead. It was a good thing Mrs. Taylor was taken up with her bird memories for she did not try to stop him from going, just sat stirring her tea slowly and looking off into space.

"We'll have tea often, Professor," she said absently. "And you'll see that those pills help you right away. Most miraculous. But mind what I say, Professor, never get a troupial bird or they'll break your heart."

He managed to get to this room and close the door before the coughing began and he thanked his lucky stars again for baseball; the sound roared out marvelously so no one could hear how the magic pills had failed him. It was a bad spell and went on and on, leaving him gasping and sweating, reaching out after the short respites for other radio stations, but none of them were as loud as baseball. He knew all the stations now from his sleepless nights in hospitals, and they were all his friends, the syrup-voiced lady MC who introduced wonderful people with wonderful mothers and wonderful songs, the buzz-saw-voiced man who answered telephones and played records from some sunken bell, the Uncle Toms and Aunt Millies who played nasal hill-billy records and would send you begonia bulbs, quilt patches, reducing pills, white Bibles, plastic aprons, incubator chickens, dahlias, doctor books, and bubble pipes on receipt of a postcard sent to this station. The night hours dragged on. Part of the time Swenstrom half dozed and the voices, turned down when he didn't need them, soothed him. In his half-dreams he thought how kind the lady on the roof had been, and he hoped she would not find out that her pills had not worked any more than anything worked nowadays. He had never done anything in his life, he thought, to deserve anyone's kindness and he was glad that Agnes had never shamed him by being too good. He thought of how much he was costing them, the expense, small as it was, of his room here and of all the doctors past and future, and how selfish his whole life had been, always taking university jobs that interested him and paid little, never considering offers of work that might have given his wife and children an easier time. Yet now in his bad days they were obliged to do for him as if it was his right, and it wasn't fair. He had had the selfish luxury of doing the work he loved, letting the family make out however they might, and he had no right now to demand any consideration. These were his night thoughts between naps.

It was almost daybreak before he began to wheeze again, cleverly dialing to the Del Rio station which was always strongest at that hour, but he remembered other people wanted to sleep so he turned it off, burying his face in the pillow, praying for the truck noises and garbage pails clanking to drown out his distress.

It was a bad attack, and no matter how he steeled himself he could never get over the wild fear of choking to death, the cowardly terror of being alone when it happened. Finally he sank back, trembling and wet with perspiration, too spent to know where or who he was, his mind floating around vacantly until he found himself thinking about the troupial bird. The bird fluttered before him, incredibly exquisite, no larger than a yellow robin with black wings and black feathery eyelashes. Swenstrom saw it clearly, and suddenly he could hear the sweet bugle call of the dear bird, piercing his heart with its song of lost homeland, lost mate, lost sky, lost treetop. Oh, poor bird! he cried out, remembering again, and he put his arm across his eyes. Look at me, he thought, an old idiot crying over a dead bird I never even saw.

ADDENDA

Dinner on the Rocks

 $\mathcal{T}$ O UNDERSTAND WHAT happened at the Dyckmanns' last Wednesday night you should know something of the
Dyckmann's attitude toward the human race. As taxi drivers di-
vide the world into fares and pedestrians, so the Dyckmanns di-
vide it into hosts and guests.

The Dyckmanns are hosts.

The instant they set foot in anyone else's house they begin to
bristle. If the party is gay they draw delicately aloof, their sensitive nostrils quivering with disapproval. When the canapés are
passed they glance over them carefully and then smilingly refuse.
At first taste of their drink they exchange a look and put it down
with quiet finality. Under cover of her fixed social smile Mrs.
Dyckmann is secretly throwing out every stick of furniture in the
host's home, burning the paintings, firing the inept servants, and
sending every stitch on the hostess's back to the thrift shop.
Meditatively twigging his iron-gray mustache Mr. Dyckmann is,

in fancy, tossing out all the guests, since everyone in anyone else's drawing room is utterly impossible. As early as possible they hasten away to wash away the unpleasant taste of other people's hospitality with their own good caviar and a really decent highball. Mr. Dyckmann's lip curls cynically at the good labels "pasted" on bottles on his friend's table.

"I give cheap liquor myself sometimes," he says later to his wife, "but at least I know what I am doing. Some people just don't know there's any difference."

It was an actual pain for the Dyckmanns to see the reins of hostmanship in any other hands but theirs. They spoke with outward disapproval of ill-bred persons who did not return invitations, but this was purely conversational. Their annoyance was not at the bad manners, but at not being given the chance to criticize an event. Their genuine sense of outrage came when someone who had been properly entertained at the Dyckmanns' had the effrontery to give a party herself.

"Good heavens, Ella Baird is having a party on the twelfth!" Mrs. Dyckmann had said four weeks ago in the tone of imagine-someone-on-relief-buying-a-television-set.

"Ella Baird?" repeated Mr. Dyckmann incredulously. "*Now* what is it?"

"A buffet," said his wife. "I suppose we'll have to go."

"That means we'll have to have them here again," sighed Mr. Dyckmann grimly, for the Dyckmanns made a point of not enjoying their own parties in the cheap way some people did. They regarded it as a hardship that you could not exhibit the rare niceties of hostmanship without having guests, but since this basic point of view was all they had in common it had become the pivot of their long marriage. As that common foe, a little child, can hold an otherwise incompatible couple together, so guests, as a common danger, had kept the Dyckmanns as one. They were in marvelous accord, for instance, in their disapproval of Ella

Baird's casual way of "springing" a party. The Bairds had lived in Chutney Hill less than a year (had it not been that Mr. Dyckmann had himself sold them their home at considerable profit the Dyckmanns would never have deigned to know them), and Ella's system of entertaining was haphazard to say the least. Feeling perhaps inadequate to choosing her own guests she was apt to adopt some friend's group *in toto*.

"Why don't you all come to my house next Sunday night for supper?" she would shriek ten minutes after she had got into somebody's home, and her hostess would feel that her own carefully planned affair was merely a rehearsal for a really bang-up wow party at Ella's, what with Ella busily passing her address around like a gypsy-tearoom card. Still Ella had such a naive enjoyment of people, and was so childishly eager to be liked, that all Chutney Hill but the Dyckmanns had to forgive her innocent piracy. "It will be fun!" she would cry as if that had anything to do with anything. The fun was often of a peculiar brand, as Mr. Baird, by way of fortifying himself against oncoming social pressure, was likely to invite a barful of strangers. The Dyckmanns feared and hated the Baird routs fully as much as the Bairds feared and respected the Dyckmann's exquisitely organized gestures. But after Ella's great orgy over the holidays with sixty guests ("Now why should they invite sixty when their house is smaller than ours, especially if they couldn't feed them anything but horse meat with creosote sauce, if you call *that* beef Strogonoff?") the Dyckmanns were obliged to put the upstarts in their place with a flying saucer inviting the Bairds for a really civilized dinner *à quatre* just to show them what should be done.

Preparations for the little dinner were made with the usual Dyckmann thoroughness, accompanied by a great deal of pious groaning since they chose to consider any contact with their fellow men a grueling test of endurance. These endless hellos and good-byes must go on, however, like plowing or threshing; somebody had to do it or there would be no crops. For a week Alice wore a patient harassed frown, planning each minute detail as if such sensational perfection would either rebuke the Bairds for their own careless standards or bring them to their feet with spontaneous cheers. "Let's not overdo," Mr. Dyckmann was obliged to remind his wife. "After all, they're only into us for one lousy buffet, and if we overdo they'll want to go us one better next time."

He was making his usual preparations for the evening by writing down a few good ones he had heard recently of the crass type he was sure would entrance Baird. These he proposed to introduce as icebreakers during the cocktails.

The Dyckmann theory of alcohol was that if guests appeared to enjoy drinking, then by all means serve very little; if they were obviously dismayed at sight of cocktail shaker or whiskey glass, then press them to indulge. The finest gin, the rarest Scotch was none too good for those lovable connoisseurs, the nonindulgers, and Mr. Dyckmann felt a genuine sense of accomplishment when he had been able to delay dinner by forcing three stiff ones on a wildly hungry teetotaler. The Bairds being hearty-drinking types, Herbert served exactly two perfectly chilled Martinis, with a gracious teaspoonful dividend, then whisked the guests into dinner the instant it was announced as if the table would take off for Gander without them if they loitered.

"What about that, old man?" Mr. Dyckmann asked proudly, showing Baird a bottle of vintage Château Mouton Rothschild he proposed to serve. Here again Mr. Dyckmann's technique was a well-thought-out caprice. If the guests were, like the Bairds, a hardy bar-rye type he pressed a fine wine upon them. If they were gourmets he knew half-a-dozen adequate little domestic vintages he begged them to agree were every bit as good as something or other.

The Bairds were somewhat ashamed of their wine-deafness and tried to show appreciation of their good fortune by sipping sturdily away, laughing loudly at Mr. Dyckmann's well-known anecdotes, Mr. Baird laughing with particular volume to cover his wife's hiccups always induced by the grape and possibly by the thorough defrosting they had done at Tom's Bar on the way over. As the oysters and then the soup were removed from the table, Herbert and Alice Dyckmann exchanged glances of achievement—three hours more and we'll be out of this—and with the roast Herbert felt fit enough to plunge into whatever subject was most disagreeable to himself, therefore undoubtedly most agreeable to his guests. While he was determinedly ducking his male guest in these desperately chosen shallows, his wife had led her female vis-à-vis out on a tightrope of gossip, both losing their balance when they hit on a common foe, but falling happily into the safety net of domestic clichés spread providentially beneath.

Everything was going properly as it always did at the Dyckmanns'. At nine-thirty Alice Dyckmann had showed Ella Baird (with the desire to instruct rather than inspire envy) some plastic doilies particularly nice for those big buffets some unfortunates gave. Ella gratefully wrote down the name of Mr. Dyckmann's wine merchant. Mrs. Dyckmann asked Ella Baird if she made all her own clothes and Ella cheerfully said that no, all she ever did was to take that junk trimming off basement dresses, add her Aunt Martha's garnets and no one ever knew the difference. At ten-thirty Mr. and Mrs. Dyckmann exchanged the delicate little preliminary yawn that to any sensitive guest was like a fire alarm. But for some reason, perhaps fooled by their pale highballs into some nonsensical idea that this was a party and that the Dyckmanns really liked them, Ella casually put her feet up on the ottoman and Baird, chuckling merrily at one of his own puns, reached over and helped himself to another fine cigar. Alarmed at this untoward liberty, hinting as it did that the guests were relaxing into a long cozy evening, Mr. and Mrs. Dyckmann mentally joined forces to remove the Bairds as expertly as they knew how. All the grim energy that had gone into building up that at-home feeling now must go into tearing it down.

"I feel more like I do now than I did when I came in," Ella quoted happily, and at the ominous words Mrs. Dyckmann lifted her left brow significantly to the maid skulking outside the door. It was the sign for ice, decanters, all glasses except those that could not be wrenched from the guests' hands, in short all evidence of liquid hospitality to vanish, the lid to be closed on bonbon and cigar box, a window to be opened down the hall letting in soothing bedroom air, as if this breeze would gently remind the Bairds as it did the Dyckmanns of counterpanes turned down, pajamas folded on eiderdowns, Nembutal bottle, Thermos of Ovaltine and night reading carefully placed on each side table, Erle Stanley Gardner for Mr. Dyckmann, Craig Rice omnibus for Mrs. Dyckmann.

Mr. Dyckmann could visualize right now the exact page on which he had left Perry Mason last night and he ached to rejoin him. The D.A.'s office had something on Perry, all right, but could they prove he was the murderer's accomplice? If the woman in the mental institution in Los Meritos was not Corinne Lansing then what had George Alder done with the body? What about the other woman whose body was washed ashore? Maddening to think that all that lay between the solution and himself were these two comfortable guests.

"Wine makes me sleepy," declared Baird, adding with a terrible laugh, "Wake me up at seven-thirty, will you, Herb?"

"Yes, we all have to get up early," said Alice Dyckmann very cleverly and her eyes were drawn longingly in the direction of the bedroom where there awaited her a select group of stylish corpses done in by a strange Burmese incense. Would the killers get Celeste, too, whom Alice had left last night innocently look-

ing over jade snuffboxes in the Galerie Orientale? Looking at
Ella's stout legs stretched out, Alice wondered peevishly why
Ella never went in for jade, and she wished devoutly it was Ella
and not lovely Celeste who was about to be conked by the suave
Burma shaver.

In crises of this sort the Dyckmanns had usually found it ef-
fective to stare into space, encouraging the long pause that might
fetch the witty words, "Well, dear, we must go." But the Bairds
were on an entirely different wavelength, and this was the fault
of the Dyckmanns. With the removal of the bottles it had been
the mutual impulse of the Bairds to shoot out the door, but their
second thought was that they must not allow such nice people as
the Dyckmanns to think their company was unbearable without
refreshment. If the Dyckmanns found it relaxing to sit around
silently staring into space, then the Bairds could take it, too,
without drink or even smoke for that matter. Ella excused herself once and went into the bedroom, but the Dyckmanns were
crushed to discover she had not gone for her wraps but to put on
fresh makeup for a possible all-night performance.

What should have been the coming of the Marines was the
sound of the hall clock striking twelve. Mr. Dyckmann, who had
often objected to the harsh, laryngeal tones of this valuable an-
tique, now regretted that the tolling of the really dangerous
hours from now on was perversely plotted by those primitive
clockmakers to create no proportionate turmoil.

"What a lovely tone," said Ella flatteringly and had seated
herself, pillow cozily thrust behind her head, when the Dyckmanns dared take fresh hope by the disappearance of Mr. Baird,
who seemed to have gone for wraps. But barely had the growling
echoes of the clock died away before there came to ear the horrible sound of laughter from the kitchen.

"Didn't Clara go to bed?" asked Mrs. Dyckmann, startled. "It
sounds as if she has company."

"It does indeed," said Mr. Dyckmann.

"Mark always gets on with the kitchen," Ella giggled, for it was indeed Mr. Baird making himself at home in the kitchen with the maid who had returned from walking the dog and was now enjoying a snack in the pantry. The banging of the icebox door, the cheerful tinkle of ice reminded Dyckmann of the unlocked liquor closet. With a reassuring nod to his wife he stalked into the kitchen. The sight of his guest at the pantry table with the cook, glasses and bottles between them, filled Mr. Dyckmann with fury.

"Come in, old man," Baird dared to call out in great good humor. "I was just teaching my old pal Clara how to make a triple header."

The idea that his otherwise-surly cook could learn anything from anybody else but her employers made the top of Mr. Dyckmann's head fairly bubble, but he commanded the muse of good manners to inspire him.

"Come back and join us in the living room, my dear man," he said quietly, and turned to his cook with a heart-chilling smile. "Clara is supposed to be off duty but I'm sure that for the sake of her old pal she'll make triple headers for all of us, eh, Clara?"

"Yes, sir," quaked Clara.

"You need three cocktail glasses apiece, you see," Baird happily explained, following Dyckmann back to the living room. "The first is the Expurgator, the second is the Extinguisher, and the third is the Exterminator. The principle comes from Boyd's Theory of Sterno-Dynamics. Wake up, Ella," he cried to his bride, "this is it."

"We're having triple headers, my dear," Mr. Dyckmann announced in a calm voice to his wife. "It's a beverage."

"It sounds very refreshing," murmured Mrs. Dyckmann, quite pale. "I hope there's Ovaltine in it."

"There isn't," said her husband shortly. Observing that he and his wife were the only ones still standing, he commanded, "Sit down, my dear."

Mrs. Dyckmann sat down, giving him a wild, betrayed look. From the kitchen came a terrific clatter and tinkle of glasses, poppings and burblings and fizzing. The sight of Mr. Dyckmann sitting on the edge of his chair, head lifted and staring straight ahead like a statue, silenced the guests' hilarity, for his face was as chalky as a circus clown's around the lips but completely purple everywhere else. Ella Baird uneasily strove to catch her husband's eye, but he could not lift his own conscience-stricken gaze from the handsome carpet. Into this silence Clara staggered with a tray of twelve brimming glasses, which she placed on the table beside Mr. Dyckmann and then with a spent sigh bolted from the room.

"The green are first, then come the amber, and last the red," explained Mr. Baird, and then coughed as he saw the frozen faces of the others. "It's—ah—it's a pretty sort of thing."

"The Expurgator," announced the host handing each a green glass. "Down, all."

Everyone shuddered except Mr. Dyckmann, who merely moistened his lips and then saw to it that the others downed theirs.

"Every drop, Alice," he reproved. "After Mr. Baird has been so good as to teach our Clara. And now the Extinguisher."

"I feel sick," said Ella Baird, fretfully taking her amber glass.

"But it's such a pretty thing," her host reminded her and again saw to it that the glasses were drained. His wife was glaring at him now for it seemed to her that whatever he was up to, it was so typical of him to make a bad situation worse, a fact she had noted on her very wedding night, thirty years ago. It was he who had chosen this chummy suburb, he who had hired Clara, he who had sold property to the Bairds, he who had encouraged this final outrage. How like him! Seeing that he was showing no sign of perturbation himself beyond turning a healthy purple in the white-lip region, she downed her Extinguisher with a smile of ineffable hatred.

"We're going a little fast," panted Baird, clutching for his wife's arm.

"What in God's name is in it, honey?" she moaned.

"It's supposed to be number one, brandy with sherry, number two, brandy with rum, number three—" Baird gasped but Mr. Dyckmann interrupted, passing him the red glass and saying, "The Exterminator, now, if you please."

"No, no," snarled Mrs. Dyckmann, but he thrust the glass sternly in her hand. It seemed to Dyckmann that of the people present he disliked Alice the most, for any other woman knew how to dispose of guests gracefully at the right moment, and any other woman would appreciate how masterly his solution of the problem was. It struck him that he could never have endured his marriage had it not been for guests and murder stories.

"The Exterminator we drink *Bruderschaft,*" muttered Baird, linking one arm through his wife's and another through Dyckmann's, a good precaution but it did not keep Ella Baird from sliding down on the large coffee table and passing out cold.

"Well, I guess we'd better say good night," said Mr. Baird vaguely. Mrs. Dyckmann looked at the lady on the table, gave her husband a long measuring look, then marched out to the bedroom. She returned with Mrs. Baird's wraps, which she adjusted on the recumbent lady as if she were dressing a corpse. Mr. Baird scratched his head with a foolish grin.

"It's been great," he said. "Mind giving me a hand with the table?"

"Not at all," said Mr. Dyckmann with alacrity and picking up the head end of the coffee table as his guest took the other end, they transported the exhausted lady to the car and slid her quite expertly into the back seat.

When Mr. Dyckmann came back in the house he was humming a classical air, something from one of the cheaper Italian operas, his wife thought as she undressed. The sounds of the motor starting persisted for some time outside and then stopped, but neither of the Dyckmanns looked out to see whether it had gone away or merely gone dead out in the cold. They nestled in their beds, they poured their Ovaltine, they opened their books.

"Shall I set the alarm?" finally inquired Mr. Dyckmann.

Slyly Mrs. Dyckmann watched him take the first sip of his Ovaltine and wondered how long it would take.

"It won't be necessary, my dear," she said. "I'll be awake."

Oh, will you now, thought Mr. Dyckmann grimly, and gave a deep sigh of content as he found his place in Erle Stanley Gardner. For there's nothing like a good murder to cheer a person up.

Can't We Cry a Little?

*A*NNA ARDELL'S SECRETARY met the committee from the broadcasting company in the alleyway of the theater. The matinee was not quite over and they stopped to smoke and confer.

"Are you sure she won't be too tired to see us after the matinee?" asked young Mr. Hartley, the program director. "We want to catch her in her best humor."

The secretary, an amiable, bald young man, shook his head. "Anna is very interested," he said. "Anna has been interested in radio for a long time. You'll find her very easy to talk to."

"Perhaps you'd better tell Mr. Caslon just what we had in mind," suggested Mr. Drew, an important radio official who had been drafted for prestige purposes. They had, as usual, embarked on this conference with the very vaguest of ideas in mind. The young program director, however, was not disconcerted.

"No use in wasting Mr. Caslon's time," he said suavely. "We'll have to explain our ideas all over to Anna. We want her as guest, to climax a series of guest stars in fifteen-minute skits. Mr. Benton here is our writer, and he has several ideas for skits for Miss Ardell. Mr. Brown produces the series. Mr. Drew, of course, you know."

The secretary nodded understandingly, as if he had received very illuminating information. Sounds of applause burst through the walls, and an usher opened the side entrance beside them, indicating the end of the matinee.

"All I suggest is this," the secretary said hastily. "Give her four ideas. Make the first historical—she hates that. Then give her two more bad ones. Save the one you want till the end. And remember, she will want to do her old vaudeville routine—you remember the clowning waitress in 'Dare I Care?' Unless you can think of some way of getting round her."

The matinee audience burst through the doors now, their faces still wreathed in their bought happiness. Mr. Drew, Mr. Benton, Mr. Brown, and Mr. Hartley tossed away their cigarettes and hastened after Mr. Caslon through the stage door.

"Tell everyone Miss Ardell is in conference," the secretary instructed the doorman, and led the way upstairs to the star's dressing room. At the door he turned back with a reassuring smile to the others. "You'll find Anna very easy to talk to," he said. "As a matter of fact, Anna is extremely interested in radio. Of course, what she really wants is her own show, not just these guest shots."

The broadcasting committee looked at one another. Mr. Caslon rapped tenderly on the dressing-room door. "Oh, Anna!" he called. "Anna dear, it's the radio people!"

"Come in!" cried a well-trained voice, and there was Miss Ardell, seated at her dressing table. She whipped out a smile of welcome, and at the same time her busy eyes appraised the delegation from the broadcasting company.

"We want you for a sketch, Miss Ardell," said Mr. Hartley, briskly. "Now, all we want is some idea of what you'd like to do. Mr. Benton here does most of our comedy skits."

Anna's eyes stripped Mr. Benton's rather large head of any comic talents and dismissed it. She flung out her long, slender, much-photographed hands in an appealing gesture.

"Must we laugh?" she pleaded. "Can't we cry a little?"

The committee looked baffled. Mr. Drew was inspired to handle this emergency.

"Miss Ardell is quite right," he said. "There is far, far too much woe in the world today for an artist to laugh. In fact, that was just what we were discussing before we came in. Mr. Hartley, our program director, will tell you the idea we had for you."

Mr. Hartley took a cigarette from a silver box. "May I?" he said, and lit it with a thoughtful air. "Suppose I just follow the routine we have at the office," he said.

Miss Ardell clasped her hands under her chin and gazed at him with the eager expectancy of a child.

"Suppose I toss out an idea and then the others shoot it full of holes. How's that? All right, here goes. The idea is this—it's a pure American theme, something that all of our listeners will cheer for—that is, it's a scene in which Martha Washington, in her bedroom at midnight, writes down in her diary her secret thoughts just before George takes office. Her hopes, her fears, her aspirations for the new country, you see."

Miss Ardell twisted her fingers over her knee, gave up the gesture as inadequate and flung her hands out as if she were quite through with the pair of them. "But the public does not think of me as that sort of national figure," she protested, her pretty brow distorted into a frown. "Martha Washington played by Anna Ardell? No, no, no. It's all wrong. It would be too big a change for me. After all, I am a comedienne. The public thinks of me as a comedienne. I don't think my manager and secretary, Mr. Caslon here, would even permit me to, would you, Cassie?"

"Frankly, gentlemen," said Mr. Caslon, dutifully, "I would rather not have Anna appear in that sort of thing."

"Tell Miss Ardell your idea, Mr. Benton," the program director said. "As a matter of fact, Mr. Benton worked on a sketch for you on the Coast last year."

"Really?" Miss Ardell turned now to Mr. Benton. It was his turn to search for a cigarette, light it, and assume an air of easy control. He began to outline a story about a willful, spoiled Southern belle, but he was interrupted.

"She sounds like such an *unpleasant,* such a *frightfully* unpleasant character," Miss Ardell said. "I couldn't—really, Mr. Benton, I *couldn't!* I mean it just wouldn't be me. I'm not a cat, I'm not a Southern belle. I'm just Annie Ardell, a little girl from home. Really, I'm a very simple person."

"Had you some idea, Mr. Drew?" the secretary asked, while Mr. Benton stammered an apology.

"I don't recall doing any sketches on the air in Los Angeles," Miss Ardell said to him, knitting her eyebrows. "You're sure you did them for me, Mr. Benton?"

The secretary turned to her. "Some material was submitted that we didn't like, Anna dear. Both times you ended up with the routine from 'Dare I Care?'"

"Mr. Drew," said the program director loudly, "I believe you had a suggestion to submit."

Mr. Drew was the oldest, best-dressed, and suavest of the callers, and it was obvious that he was highest in authority. Anna's eyes, a faded-overall blue, rested on him. "I have such faith in the radio," she said wistfully. "There are so many, many things one can do there. Big things—things so terribly, terribly worth while. These usual little sketches—Martha Washington, Queen Victoria, divorced-wife stuff, Southern belle"—she did not look at Mr. Benton, but he blushed properly—"they all seem so dreadfully trivial, so—do you see what I mean?—so commonplace. When you think of—I mean, what really, truly can be done by a person—oh, I don't mean me, not me, necessarily, but by some big artist, a truly great artist, one with vision, you know." She threw up the hands again prettily and then clasped them in laughing excitement. "But I mustn't be so serious about it. And it's you people who know best, after all. It's your business."

"No, no," protested Mr. Drew. "It's you and artists like you who make radio. Now, take Baby Snooks—"

"Amusing, delightful, of course," said Miss Ardell with a pained smile, "but I'm not a Baby Snooks, Mr. Drew. If you knew me, you would know that it is the little sad things, just tiny little things, really, that move me most. Laugh, yes. But tears— aren't they important, Mr. Drew?"

"Then why not do 'Old Rose'?" demanded Mr. Drew. "Tell her about 'Old Rose,' Hartley. It's a script we just bought."

"A beautiful script," said the program director. "Old Rose is an old scrubwoman. We use Strauss waltzes for musical bridges and break up the story at five points in her life..."

....

When he finished, Miss Ardell's eyes were moist. "So very humble," she said, "And so really good. Just the simple life of a very good person, isn't it?"

"It's perfect for you," ventured Mr. Drew.

"And she is poor?" Miss Ardell asked.

"Very poor," the program director assured her.

"But she thinks she has been wicked to enjoy life so much," Mr. Brown said. "Sunshine, flowers, trees, birds—she thinks she has been rich in these and enjoyed them more than others."

"Sweet!" said Miss Ardell, winking back tears. "Oh, I must do that! Cassie dear, it's exactly what I have been looking for. Now, now, you see? All we needed was to talk it over."

The broadcasting committee rose as their hostess leaped to her feet and clasped all their hands warmly. Mr. Caslon bowed to them. There was a busy interchange of cigarettes and matches and the usual difficulty in organizing for departure. Miss Ardell tucked her arm through Mr. Caslon's.

"Oh, Cassie, it's good! It's *good!*" she cried softly. "Five different characters, really, and all so moving, don't you see? it does something to you. Even the title, 'Old Rose.'"

"It gets you," Mr. Caslon agreed.

The program director buttoned his coat complacently. "I knew we'd find the right thing if we just got together," he said.

"It's the kind of thing that will make an entirely new public for you, Miss Ardell," Mr. Drew said from the doorway.

"A public that doesn't think you can do anything besides the old 'Dare I Care?' sort of thing." Mr. Benton smiled.

"Not that your public ever gets tired of that," Mr. Brown said cautiously.

"No, no, indeed!" said Mr. Benton. "People all over the world love you for that routine alone."

At this, the artist's slim, overwrought hands flew to her temples. "Oh, Cassie, Cassie, I'm afraid it won't do," she exclaimed. "It just won't work. Mr. Brown and Mr. Benton are right. Everyone will insist on 'Dare I Care?' They expect it of me. I'll have to do it, Cassie darling. That's all there is to it. They love it!"

"But, Anna darling, you've done it dozens of times on the air," said Mr. Caslon gently. "Everyone knows the whole thing by heart."

"No," said Miss Ardell. "I'll have to do it once more. It breaks my heart, but—well, I just couldn't bear to disappoint so many people. Good-bye, gentlemen. Thanks so much. I do hope it works out."

The broadcasting committee walked somberly down the rickety steps and out into the alleyway. They stood there for a moment, waiting for the secretary. In a little while he clattered down the stairs behind them and emerged, hatless and breathless.

"Anna's very happy about the whole thing," he said.

"Splendid!" said Mr. Drew. "A delightful person to meet."

"No side to Anna," said Mr. Caslon. "Just a nice kid."

"I trust we didn't exhaust her," added Mr. Drew.

"We merely wanted to get exactly the right idea for her," said the program director.

Mr. Caslon shook his head. "But, boy, you radio fellows are tough ones to please!" He sighed. "I never saw anyone beat Anna down like that before."

The program director acknowledged this with a pleased shrug. "It's a strict medium," he said, "a very strict medium."

The Elopers

$\mathcal{J}$N THE SUNKEN GARDEN the scarlet geraniums bloomed, and the weeping willows dripped pale green branches along the graveled paths. Trees and grass seemed far greener here than in Manhattan, across the bridge. It was only June, but here on Ward's Island the summer might have been at its ripest. The lush green lawns, the vine-covered porches of the little gingerbread houses, the blossoming country lanes, so tranquil and remote from the city, seemed, under the great stone bridges, to be a lovely buried village of long, long ago. The stern new buildings on the edge were tall sentries, guarding the hush within.

In the bus shed Alma overheard someone remark on the beauty of the grounds, and a woman's tired voice answered, "It's pretty, all right, but you get so you're afraid of beautiful grounds like this. It's always an orphanage or a poorhouse or a prison. I'll bet the ones who have to stay here would be happier in the heart of the slums or in a factory town. At least there'd be life."

It was long past visiting hours, which meant a long wait for the bus back to 125th Street. At least she wouldn't have to stand. Coming over, the young athletes bound for Randall's Island always grabbed the seats, shoving aside the weary old mothers laden with hampers for the hospital patients. Alma recognized two of the women waiting in the shed, those who had probably stayed, as she had, to confer with the doctors. There was the pretty, dark woman who came over every week to visit her old music teacher, "the Maestro," as she called him.

"Today I sang for the Maestro and he *knew,* he really did," she whispered to Alma. "He said, 'How many times must I tell you to come *up* on that note, not pounce on it?' Just like his old self!"

A small gray woman with her canvas carryall on her lap had been coming here as many years as Alma had, and nodded to her.

"I thought you had taken your son home," Alma said. "Wasn't he discharged?

"He always has to come back," the woman said with a shrug. "Outside gets too much for him after three, four weeks. He can't understand. No friends anymore, nothing to do, no place to go, and me away all day. My mother's in the apartment, but she's old and keeps at him, do this, do that. So he eloped."

"Eloped?"

The woman smiled.

"They call it eloping, running away from the hospital," she said. "He was always in trouble with the doctors, always trying to elope back to the Bronx. Then they'd catch him and put him in a closed ward. Only this time—it's funny, isn't it?—he eloped back to Ward's instead of away. Some do that. When they can't stand up to something they got to elope."

"Well, at least he made his own decision," Alma consoled her.

"If only he could see it that way," said the other. "Your daughter went to staff, didn't she? Does that mean you're taking her home at last?"

"Her father's bringing her home tomorrow," she said. "She's going to be all right now. Those marvelous new drugs! I just brought a new outfit for her, and she was so thrilled. Full of plans, of course."

"You brought her here the same time I brought Max," the woman remembered. "Six years."

"It's been so long," Alma said. "I'm the one that's scared."

The woman knew.

"I'm telling you," she said.

The bus came along and the three women climbed on, taking separate seats with their separate problems to solve, their separate canvas bags. The bags told the story. There was a time when Alma would see someone carrying one of those cram-full bags on a summer Sunday and she'd think it meant a picnic, a beach outing. Now, whenever she saw a woman carrying one, she wondered what hospital she was headed for, how far she had come, how many weeks or years she had been carrying it. Her own bag today contained the clothes Deedee had on when they brought her here from Bellevue that sad summer day. A size nine then, she had grown taller and stouter and now looked old for her nineteen years. Her fair hair, newly curled at the island beauty shop where she had been working lately, was still beautiful. Even in her most depressed state Deedee had been vain, brushing her hair all day long. Another good thing: Her eyes were alive again. Some of them never got over the fixed, wide-eyed stare, even when they were well, but Deedee's eyes were warm and alert, clouding up quickly, oh yes, when something puzzled her or something was denied her. There were so many things she had been denied, and now that she was coming out the poor child expected everything to be waiting for her—the skates, the cocker spaniel, the guitar with lessons, the electric sewing machine, the fur skating boots, the chocolate almond cake.... Alma took her memo pad out of her purse and wrote "chocolate cake" on her list.

She looked out over the river, the river that had seemed to her the dividing line between hope and despair. Today it was jeweled with sunset colors and the reflected lights of the highway; even the tugs seemed beautiful, because Deedee was coming home, Deedee was going to be all right.

The old doctor himself had acknowledged that she could have gotten out long ago.

"She was one of the half dozen out of a hundred I could have helped, maybe cured," he had said angrily. "But time is what you have to give them, and in my job here I have to see two hundred patients a day. Time, time is what we need and what do they give us—buildings! None of *their* doing we get these bright young doctors coming over to save somebody once in a while! Your good luck, Mrs. Davis."

It was indeed, Alma admitted. The new young doctor had taken a personal interest in Deedee's painting and dress designs. He had several paintings by patients hanging in his office, and Deedee's, the gleaming white sight-seeing boat steaming up the blue river toward Hell Gate, was his favorite. Alma did not like to look at the other paintings, the one of the huge cavern with jagged gray rocks and pitch-black water below, or the one with the twisted dead tree, its branches hung with blood-red blossoms, black roots curling back up around the trunk instead of going into the ground. There was a haunting self-portrait of a woman, a long greenish-white drowned face with black hair floating off into midnight-blue clouds, long snaky throat drifting on marble-white waves. The eyelids were closed, and when Alma exclaimed about this, the doctor said that schizophrenics invariably painted themselves with closed eyes. But Deedee's pictures were outgoing, joyous, he said. There was every chance for her, he said.

On her memo pad Alma wrote "drawing pad."

The conversation of the two men on the seat behind her came into her consciousness.

"Four years isn't so bad," one was saying. "Me, I've been visiting my wife here for thirty years. Can you take yours home weekends?"

"I can't, even if they'd let me," the other said. "She doesn't know the apartment's gone and I'm in a rooming house. She worries about my mending and getting the right meals, as it is. I tell her the reason I have time to visit her on Wednesdays, too, is that the boss is so understanding. Hell, I lost my job three months ago. Too much on my mind. She's better, though. Helps in the hospital laundry, watches TV, plays bingo. She almost always knows me now."

"I sold our house as soon as we got my wife here," the older man said. "Private doctors had used up all the insurance before that. I've kept my job, but that means I have to pay board for her here till I'm retired, so it doesn't leave me much. I couldn't take her home now even if she was well. Nobody to look after her. Nobody even remembers her."

Alma thought of the miracle in her own life and breathed a sigh of immense gratitude. Her last trip on this fateful bus. No more hearing all around her the voices of strangers telling each other, or maybe only themselves, the way it was, always how there was no one else who cared. No more would her heart flip when the bus left the line of cars from the Triborough Bridge headed for Queens and zoomed down through the underpass to the lost island. It was like a ship taking off for outer space, she always felt. But now Deedee was coming back from the island of the moon.

"You can't skip a visit, no," the older man's voice went on. "No one else ever comes. I guess everybody's got their own problems."

"But not even a pack of cigarettes from her own brother," the other said. "Not even a card."

"You get used to it." said the older man. He had a deep, cheerful voice, and when his companion got off at Second Avenue, Alma turned to look at him. He had iron-gray hair and a trim mustache, with a furrowed, ruddy, good face. Settling back alone in his seat, the warm glow faded from his eyes, and she saw him staring out the window with a look of deep, dark loneliness. At 125th Street he was the first to get off, and she watched him marching toward the subway, his shoulders back, jauntily swinging his blue-plaid bag, pausing at the newsstand to buy a paper. She wondered where... but no, she reminded herself, she no longer needed to wonder about all the others. She was free.

She celebrated her new freedom by taking the Lexington Avenue bus down, instead of the subway, because now there was time; life was beginning again. She even felt a vague pang that she might never see this corner of New York again. She looked about her with her new eyes, good-bye eyes, and felt the old joy of the city, its special magic of transforming the familiar by rain or moon or new street lights. Surely she had taken this same bus a hundred times before, but today, bewitched by the miracle of Deedee, she saw out of her window a new world, foreign and magical. She spelled out the shop signs—*Café*, *Bodega*, *Carniceria*, *Joyeria*—and smiled, wishing Walter were along to be reminded of their Caribbean honeymoon. The dingy, crumbling old brownstone houses along upper Lexington, so wretched by day, blazed open by lamplight in brilliant detail, as if their facades were transparent black veils. On the doorsteps, dark, laughing young men plucked guitars; on the street, older men sat on boxes having their shoes shined and watching the girls go by. Saturday night in Spanish Harlem. Doors swung open on lighted staircases down which dark young girls in pink and blue lace and gleaming satin, hair decked with jeweled flowers, danced to the street. Alma caught a glimpse of a side street bannered with a rainbow of dresses, toys, balloons, stretching a chain of golden lights westward to the medieval-looking arches of the Grand Central tracks. Like an old Spanish town, she would tell Walter. She strained her eyes to drink in the vivid vignettes among the patches of darkness.

The glaring ceiling lights opened up interiors to her as if by a powerful camera. There were shots of families, standing around a piano, gathered around a card table. It dawned on Alma that in each picture there was a close-up of a young girl standing apart, head lifted defiantly, delivering her declaration of independence. She was going to leave home, she was going to marry Pablo, she was going to have this and have that.... The shadowy faces of the girls blended into one fair, proud little face—Deedee's. As the bus rolled on below 100th Street leaving the gaudy glitter of the foreign world for the hostile, bleak fortresses of "projects" and civilization, Alma came back to the thought of Deedee. Tomorrow night, probably at this very hour, Deedee would be home.

"Get blue satin hair band," Alma jotted down on her list.

Her own room all trimmed in blue, Deedee had asked, her own drawing desk, a blue satin dress with shoes to match, and don't forget the black cocker spaniel. Alma shivered, remembering all the impossible things she had promised, reassuring herself that there must certainly be a day when the money would start coming in again instead of always going out. But now the years were up and Deedee was coming home to collect.

If only the bus ride could last a little longer, Alma thought, she might be able to think of the right thing to do. She got off at 80th Street and walked slowly eastward. The city was hotter than the island, but they were near enough to the river to get a breeze and, even though their basement was dark, it was cooler than their old apartment. She opened the iron gate and went down the steps to their entrance.

Walter was stirring a dish on the "efficiency" unit in the corner of the living room and the room smelled of frankfurters and beans, their traditional Saturday-night supper. He had laid the cloth on the card table with the little shaker of Martinis as centerpiece.

"You're late, so I'm two ahead of you," Walter said. "Take a look at the room: see what you think."

Alma went to the curtained-off alcove where Deedee was to sleep. Walter had been fixing it up for days, building in bookshelves, attaching a wall desk, making a false window out of a mirror, with blue plastic curtains to match the cot. She saw that he had placed a tiny black toy dog in the middle of the cot.

"Deedee will love it!" she said.

Walter poured her a drink and refilled his own glass. He was fair, like Deedee, his hair white now but his face still boyish.

"I hope you braced her for the piano being gone," he said.

"The doctor scolded me for not preparing her enough," Alma admitted. "But, darling, how could I? I couldn't have told her all those years when she couldn't reason! And since she's been getting well, she's had her heart so set on things I couldn't bear to bring her down to earth; I could just hope that we'd have some kind of luck before she got out."

"Everything all set for tomorrow?" he asked.

"All set," Alma said. "She's happy. Wants to go to a lot of movies, see Radio City Music Hall, take a course in dress designing, learn to drive a car."

"I'll take her to the Music Hall the minute she gets in," Walter said. "At least we can do that."

"I'll take her to the museum Tuesday to see the costumes," Alma said. "If she has something different to think about every day, it will give us time to figure out how to manage."

"Oh, it'll work out," Walter said. "The great thing is that she's come through and we're going to have her back home at last."

He poured the last of the shaker into her glass. Alma's eyes strayed to the half-filled bottle put away on the shelf for tomorrow.

"Let's drink tomorrow's now," she said. "The way we always do."

What Are You Doing in My Dreams?

𝒯HE BEST TIME TO RUN away is September. When you run away in July the good people are off someplace else. Their daughters or wives are on guard, and one of them will be blocking the front door, arms folded, yelling at you, "Where do you think you're going, missy, with that suitcase? If you think you're going to throw your clothes around my house you got another think coming." What you have to do is to walk right on down the street, keeping your eyes straight ahead, pretending you're on your way someplace a lot better.

And that's the way it turns out, too; wherever you land is sure to be better than the place you left.

I found that out the first time I ran away. I was four and the running away wasn't my own idea at all. My sister and her girl-friend, who were nearly six, found a stack of old colored circus handbills in the woodshed and they dressed me up in them over my pantywaist. Then they led me to the middle of the road and said, "Here's a comb for you to play 'Yankee Doodle' on. Go ahead, now, and be a parade."

I was scared stiff but at the same time proud at being given this assignment. I started marching, playing "Yankee Doodle" on the comb big as you please. They followed me until I turned down a forbidden corner and then it was their turn to get scared. I could hear them running back home shouting to my mother that I was running away again but I couldn't turn back now. I went on marching one-two-one-two down the center of the dusty, unknown road till I came to a tiny gingerbread house set on a steep grassy bank. My legs were wobbling but I marched up the stairs, stopping at the landing to mark time one-two-one-two in case anyone was watching. A lacy white trellis decorated the front porch and there I stopped in my tracks, for hanging from the ceiling was a shining birdcage with a beautiful golden bird in it, a real bird, singing. I could not take my eyes from it, but sank down on the stoop, my skirt of billposters crackling under me, filled with such rapture as I had never known. When the lady came out and spoke to me I burst into fierce sobs, not because she laughed at my paper dress or because she was taking me home to a certain spanking, but because I wanted to stay with the golden bird the rest of my life.

I had my own good reason for running away the next time, when I was eleven. We were on a farm with a new stepmother who didn't know what to do with us so she put us outdoors after breakfast and locked all the doors. But we couldn't go in the barn because she said it would bother the horses. We couldn't play in the orchard because we'd spoil the fruit. We couldn't go for a walk because we'd wear out our shoes. We couldn't sing our songs because the racket would keep the hens from laying. We couldn't read our old schoolbooks because we'd dirty them. However, unknown to her, we had discovered a pile of brown ledgers and colored pencils in a burned old cabin in the fields. My sister drew pictures and I wrote poems and stories. I must have knocked off a hundred poems and a dozen historical novels all romantically involving brave Colonial maidens and rich, titled Redcoats. Since our creative labors made no noise, we were happily undiscovered for a good fortnight.

Then one day the ledgers vanished from their hiding place under the kitchen porch.

"No use looking," our stepmother called out from the other side of the locked screen door. "I burned all that trash you were writing."

So I ran away. I didn't give her the money I made picking berries that week but used the whole ninety cents traveling to a startled aunt's house in the next county.

"But just what in the world did she do to you?" they all kept asking me. "Did she beat you?"

"She called my notebooks trash," I had to keep telling them over and over.

A person almost loses their patience trying to get some simple little thing through a grown-up's head.

My aunt's house was a fine place with a piano instead of a golden bird. I learned to play *Très Moutarde* and decided that the next place I ran away to would be New York City, but it was eight years more before I made it. Even then it was by way of a farm that had paid my railroad fare and given me board in exchange for "farmeretting." There's something about farm life that gives you the strength to run anywhere in the world. Oh, there were always people to tell me I'd be sorry, strangers wouldn't make allowances for me the way my own folks would if I didn't make good; I'd be homesick. But whenever I left I shut the door on that place and was never sorry, nor did I ever miss anybody I left.

But you wait, you'll miss Ohio, they all said; it's in your blood, six generations of it. You'll see. They told me how real Ohioans can sense the instant they've crossed the state border. Maybe a person has been thousands of miles away, never thinking about old Richland County or Ashtabula or wherever. Comes a time he's on the Broadway Limited, fast asleep in his lower berth when suddenly he's wide awake, snaps his fingers and says, "We're in Ohio," and sure enough! Once it almost happened to me, at that. I was on a sleeper traveling west from New York when I woke up all of a sudden for no reason. I knew I was in Ohio. My heart began thumping with a kind of terror, the terror of discovering you're human, which is worse than any fear of the supernatural. This is it, I thought, that Ohio feeling that is stronger than willpower or reason.

I yanked up the window shade and saw level fields stretching endlessly to a skimpy fringe of tall, long-legged trees far away against the pearly dawn sky. Hickory trees! Tears came to my eyes. Ohio hickories! So it was really true, I marveled, there were unknown dimensions beyond logic, a blood-knowledge. How had I dared to doubt it! Then the station came into sight and I blinked hard. What angered me the most was the goofy readiness with which I had accepted the mystique of Ohio blood and the outraged incredulity with which I fought the simple scientific fact that we were in Erie, Pennsylvania.

You might argue that a little fact like Erie, Pennsylvania, need not upset the essential truth of the theory. You could say I should not have looked out the window but should have been content to believe. If I'd just waited an hour longer before looking out it would have been Ohio all right. Nonetheless, I muttered bitterly, and after letting me down like this you won't catch me going back.

"You'll have to come back," my sister had warned me. "You can not fight it. Your family is your family."

"I'm not a family person," I said. "I'll never give them a thought."

That's where the joke was on me. Over the years this one died and that one, but I never went back to funerals. So they're dead, so the past is dead, and Ohio is gone. All right. Today is here. New York is here. Why go back to the dead?

Why indeed? The way it's turned out I haven't needed to. For the dead all come to me.

Do you know how some people's lives seem to stop like a clock at a certain mark? They go on living, get married, have families, save money, travel around the world, trade in their cars and houses and jobs, but all that is their dead life. Their life really stopped the year they were captain of the high-school football team, the year they had the lead in the college play, the day they quit Paris or the army or the newspaper job. Other jobs and mates come and go, babies grow up and have babies, the exercise horse is mounted each day as if it was really going somewhere, but all the time the rider is transfixed in an old college song or in Tony's speakeasy or in that regiment.

You can run into one of these frozen riders on the street after twenty years and if you belong in that old picture he will pounce upon you with delight, cling to your hands for dear life, introduce you ecstatically to his companion. There is nobody in the world he's gladder to see, he shouts, and before you can open your mouth he's off telling anecdotes about I'll-never-forget-the-time, keeping you buttonholed on a windy corner for half an hour, a stage prop for his monologue.

When he gets home he can't wait to tell his wife guess-who-he-ran-into, of all people, and does she remember the time... But before he can repeat all the same old stories, she interrupts to ask how you looked, what were you doing now, where were you living? Why, he doesn't know, he says, giving her a wounded look, hurt that she doesn't share his sentimental love of an old pal. The truth is he didn't even see you after the first flash of recognition; you could have been on crutches or rattling a tin cup, selling shoelaces for all he saw. What he was so glad to see was himself twenty years ago scoring that touchdown or being that cracker-jack reporter. The only thing Old Softie is really soft about is Old Softie.

In a way something like that happened to me when I ran away from Ohio. People and places froze into position and nothing I've seen or heard of them since makes any impression on that original picture. It isn't that I'm crazy about the picture or even that I dislike it. It's just that I live in that picture, whether I want to or not, when I fall asleep at night.

It's as if the day I left Ohio I split in two at the crossroads, and went up both roads, half of me by day here in New York and the other half by night with the dead in long-ago Ohio. This has been going on so many years I wonder how I survive. How tired you can be in the morning after a night with the dead!

The dead never get tired. They always have to be on the go, and no matter how I beg to be let alone, the minute I close my eyes, there they are tugging at me, pulling me along on the picnic, my grandmother yanking one of my arms as if it were a chicken wing, my Aunt Dawn holding the other. Or else my sister and I are hanging onto an eternal picnic hamper, half carrying it and half carried along, for it almost floats by itself.

It's always a picnic or a shore dinner when you're out with the dead in my family. You would think they would have had enough chicken and potato salad and oyster pie after all those family reunions, and considering that their stomachs had killed most of them, but no, it's always the same. The basket's packed, here we go. Look, it's going to rain, I whimper; see how gray the sky is, do let me stay in bed. I'm so sleepy, so tired, and you all go so fast! But they pay no attention.

In dreams the sky is always gray, anyway, like the world seen through a chicken's eyes or so they say, and it's a very low sky, with hardly enough headroom even for us children. The grass is gray, too, as we run along just above it, feet not touching it, only I'm always stumbling because they hurry me along pell-mell. Always we have to be somewhere or we'll miss something; we must rush to catch the bus or the train that has no engine, or we must hitch up those horses I never see, and everything is whispering "Hurry, hurry, hurry." Everybody knows the plan, where we are going, and what we're to do—everybody but myself. Pilgrim Lake, Cooney's Grove, Put-in-Bay, Puritan Springs, Grange Park, all blend. Everybody knows which side of the trolley tracks to wait on except stupid me and which direction the car will come from. There is always a brass band in picnicland, although I never hear it. All I ever see is an empty bandstand (but it isn't empty, I know) with bunting draped around it. In one dream my sister let go my arm when we came to the bandstand and started painting her cheeks by wetting some of the red bunting (she always knew how to do things!)—a sure sign she was going to start flirting with the band boys.

"It's not nice for you to use rouge," I protested, shocked. "It doesn't look right for a dead girl."

Sometimes when I say the word "dead" the dream is over, but more often nobody pays any attention, we're in such a big hurry. My stockings fall down, my petticoat drops, my shoes are unlaced, my hair ribbon is lost, my side hurts from running; all I want is to lie down in the grass but no one will let me. The shore dinner, they whisper, hurry, hurry, hurry, hang on to the basket, pull up your stockings, pull down your dress, straighten your sash, the shore dinner, hurry, hurry, hurry. Stop being so bossy, I wail, don't you know I've run away from all of you, I don't belong to you anymore, I've shut that door the way I always do, you needn't think you can take over my life, pushing me around in my sleep. Talk about Greenwich Village trash pestering me to whoop it up with them all night. What about dead trash forcing me to whoop it up all over hell and gone night after night? And while we're at it, why can't we go somewhere I want to, if we've got to go, and this time let's invite everybody, let it be my treat!

But it's always got to be their show. Sometimes my father shows up, eager to go. This I dread, for all the women start picking on him right away, and even though he's just as dead as they are he's never allowed to come along. He looks so disappointed that I want to cry out, "Never mind, Papa, the basket never gets opened up, we never really get there, and it's only a dream anyway."

Sometimes a new face appears, someone fresh from yesterday's obituary page, a New York friend, and this is a problem. It's hard to mix friends with family, live or dead, and I'm torn between them. Wait for me at the corner bar till I get rid of the folks, I whisper to Niles or La Touche or Gene or Jacques, I won't be forever. Wait for me and I'll tell you how I ran away from home.

But they fade away, smiling faintly. I don't hold it against them. Who wants to meet a 1910 Ohio child carrying a basket lunch in a dead man's saloon?